Working in a government s‹
my dream job; it had plenty oт perks and flexible
working hours. That was until the indescribable
happened. One of the other scientists in the facility
thought they had found a cure for all diseases known to
mankind. They said it was a scientific breakthrough.
According to them, they had found an invisible nucleus
that could change a person's cell structure within the
human body. I wondered at the time what chemicals
were used to make it such a potent drug. The facility
itself was a humongous testing area with the latest high-
tech equipment that was built to last a lifetime. The
Government built the compound in the 1940s in the
eventuality that nuclear war would break out. A safe
hold, they called it.

Volunteers from the army were the first to be tested on.
Soldiers were told they would be immune and would
receive a thousand dollars for their co-operation. They
didn't know what was to happen. When they first started
with the trial runs, the effects of the drugs were so
potent that they killed off the red blood cells in the
body, hence the soldiers died. The government then
turned to the public, looking for people that didn't
matter. They took people off the streets and enticed
them with the offer of a warm bed and a good meal.
Little did they know what was to happen?

Remembering the first time was terrible; as I read it in
the notes in the years that followed. They took it upon
themselves to test the new wonder drug on a young
man. One of the head scientists tied him to a bed; they
must have sedated him, as he was way too cooperative.

The assistants were told to keep him under close observation, but within hours, the transition had taken effect. Instead of drugs working, it changed him. The young man shook like his body was on fire. He became aggressive, his muscles increased and his facial features changed. Skin peeled off his face and fresh skin grew back in a matter of seconds. Fangs grew in place of normal teeth. After he transitioned, he was no longer human. He was a creature. The creature broke free from its restraints and started to attack the scientists within hours. He had spread the virus from one man to the next. He bit into their necks, drinking their blood like a wild animal, satisfying himself with each victim before moving on to the next. The creatures left a sickening smell of death in the air.

The facility's security tried to use smoke bombs and firearms to control the infected, but nothing had any effect on them. They still came; the creatures roamed the compound, taking full control. On the day this tragic incident happened, I was working in the lab on a theory of how human hormones could interact with the cells of a plant when I heard a tremendous explosion from a distinct part of the facility. I went to look even though I had a bad feeling, a sense of foreboding raised within me. Shaking like a leaf, I opened the doors to the lab, peering down the long, dark, narrow corridor. My eyes widened, focusing on the bloody handprints that were smeared on the walls.

The feelings within me and the evidence I saw made it very obvious that indeed something awful had taken place. I froze. Feeling a deep sense of a presence, of something behind me, I whirled around with the fear of God in me, and immediately I saw its sharp teeth, with fangs that dripped with blood. The thing stared at me with red piercing eyes before attacking me. The pain was horrendous as it sank its teeth into my neck. And then I noticed Mark Speller's walking cane with the best cherry wood handle, with a silver tip. Mark was an extraordinary gentleman. He was in his late 60s but full of so many stories. He had visited places for their monumental history, the temples of India, The Egyptian Tombs, including the Great Wall of China.

Grabbing the cane, I plunged it into the creature's chest cavity. He fell backward in shock. Clutching its chest, he landed on a nearby table. Whilst he was lying there, I took my chance and made my escape. I was clutching at my neck wound. Dying with no one there scared the shit out of me. I didn't want to be alone in what may have been my last moments. I had to leave the facility before the creature came at me again. Run, my mind said. Run. My face was wet with sweat, blood was streaming down my neck, mixing with my necklace and my sweat, and I knew then I was going to pass out. I had to see how bad it was. I wept. I was dying alone. I felt dizzy and sick. It was like a scene from a horror show, but this time I was the main character. I rushed into the bathroom nearest the stairs. I looked in the long curved-shaped mirror. My ebony hair was in a mangled mess. Sweat dripped down my face from the adrenaline that was pulsating through my veins. My black eyeliner had turned into a small pool of darkness. I lifted my hand to see two gaping holes and a lot of dark blood on my neck.

Making my way out of the bathroom, I went down the stairs; I didn't give myself a chance to look back, and all I could do was sob. I left the screams behind me.

Marching through the dense woodland of tall trees, where the smell of cherry wood and old oak trees heightened my senses with delight. As I drifted through the forest, I could feel the veined olive roughness of the branches whipping at my face. Most of the forest had been flooded from the intense rain we had in the last few weeks. The ground was a moistened, mucky bog. Carrying on, running through the woods, the crescent moon lit my way as it shined like a silvery glow, and the stars stretched on forever. I remembered my 18th birthday. I had spent it in this forest with John Horncastle; I surrendered my virginity to him that night and even then I felt I was being watched. I thought he loved me. I remembered we carved our names into old oak trees. We wanted it to last forever. The following day, he was found dead. Someone had ripped him apart. They said it was a wild animal in the papers, but now I think otherwise.

Feeling better, I felt like nothing could hurt me. The warmth of the wind brushed my soft pale skin, and the ground felt like I was running on soft fluffy clouds of candyfloss, and then everything went black. Waking up, I lay on a thick, crisp blanket of soggy leaves. I raised myself against an old tree stump; it must have been a cherry wood in its day as it still left a lingering odor. I noticed a few things about myself. I felt almost invincible and the pain from a bad back was gone. I felt amazing. Touching my body, I realized my skin felt ice-cold, like a frozen pond in winter. I was glad to still be wearing my necklace though, for some reason, I couldn't bear losing it.

Sniffing the air, I smelt a mixture of smells, from the old dead trees to the sweet smell of flesh. That got me thinking even more. What was I? What had I become? I looked around to see if anyone was watching me. Touching my neck, you would think I would feel intense pain, but nothing, yet it felt smooth and cold. Feeling suspicious, I opened my mouth and touched my teeth; sharp and pointy, come to mind, like that of a vicious bloodhound. I couldn't help but remember the last television show that I had watched. My mind was telling me I resembled the creatures that were in it. The creatures were sparkling like glitter and there were a lot of young people having sex. I knew it then. Fuck, I was a goddamn vampire!

Chapter 2

Within the following week, I had moved into an old abandoned gun shop. I discovered it had a cool-looking basement. They must have used it as an old shelter bunker in the last war. It still had pictures of vintage half-naked women pinned to the walls. As I continued to search the place, I found old tins of baked products. I went back outside; I noticed something that piqued my interest. Outside on the road stood a mean-looking motorbike, seductively I wiped my hand over it, maybe more like a caress, what a babe! It was a Harley Davidson all in black. Well, she will do very nicely for me. I wondered if she still ran. I couldn't find the keys so I hot-wired it. Oh yeah, she sounded great and fortunately for me, had a full tank of juice to make the find complete. I smiled as I took it for a spin. I eventually returned to the gun shop. I knew I had to finish setting up camp. I made a makeshift lab in the back room of the basement. Scientific work can take time. I've been trying to reverse the effects of the virus, that's what I call it, but nothing is adding up. I guess I will carry on looking for supplies. I hunt for anything that can be useful. Outside, it's getting harder to hunt. Every time I go out there, someone or something is pursuing me, either another revengeful vamp hunting for my blood or the bloody military with their guns. Whilst I searched the gun shop for equipment, I found two samurai swords. They had a great age to them, ancient maybe. Either way, they would make me feel a lot safer.

Two years later

The world had gone into meltdown. The city's infrastructure had lost its ability to sustain power. Clean drinking water had become a valuable commodity for all. The city's mall had become a trader's paradise for vampires and humans alike. Walking through the mall, the smell coming from different stalls heightened my senses; smells of flesh caused me to salivate, to lick my lips. People brushed past me and it was then I caught the distinction between different cultures, and smells that make me dream of foreign travels and paradise with its white sands and ocean blue skies. One smell I inhaled was from a stall that was selling medicines and potions. I would investigate this at a later date. I detected one distinctive scent in the air, very particular; it hit me with a smell I loved, fresh flesh. I dribbled for a brief moment, even though I loved the smell, yet the thought of eating humans made me want to puke. Walking on I wondered why this flea pit was still selling body parts, they had been warned to stop selling dodgy meat by the vampire cops as it was making vamps die. I thought about destroying it for them, but considering my options; the dick heads supplying the meat would just kill more homeless people, and more and more would go missing. I walked past, glaring at the stall owner. A man with sunken eyes and a smell of garbage was serving a human. That got me even more suspicious. He noticed me looking.

"I don't want any trouble; I'm just doing my job," he said.

Giving him a dirty look, I walked on. I figured I would be back later. I walked past the many stalls that sold fine fur coats from Milan, clean drinking water from the farthest rivers of the Amazon, and more. Finally, I came upon the stall that sold dead animals. Passing the guy some fags we then traded... He sniffed at them as if they were fake cigarettes.

"What you after?" He said in a deep, grumpy voice.

Inspecting what he had on the stall. I stated I wanted fresh steaks from the freshest cow he had. The guy looked at me before passing me the meat. You have never seen a vamp who loves cow meat, I thought. I walked away, admiring my meat package. Heading back to the gun shop, I was thinking about the crimes on the streets. Organized crime had been on the rise. The vamps that turned intelligent gave street gangs control over different sectors of the city. They all answered to an underground organization, run by several head vamps, all of which controlled the riches of the city. Money always talks. It can buy you whatever you want, yes, even death itself. Heading back to the gun shop I felt anger. I may be a stinking vamp, but I still had my morals, and I fucking hated the big shots. One day, I will kill them all.

Dropping my supplies, I prepared some food. After eating my fill, I headed out once again. Looking at the bright moon left me with a warm feeling, a feeling of belonging. It was truly an amazing night. Climbing back on my motorbike I let out a sigh. There were things from the world before that I had missed, places that I visited, like the lakes with my parents. In the weeks after the virus spread, I went to visit them, hoping my parents would still be alive, but my parents were dead. There they were, just lying on the carpet of the living room floor, holding hands with their necks torn out. I admit I cried, and it was then I wanted revenge and hated vampires even more. Oh yes, I wanted bloody revenge.

My parents were loved by everyone. They helped with cake sales for the local church; they hosted a splendid party and invited everyone in. My father was an ex-boxer called the Great Mere; everybody loved him for his character and the way he loved to help others in the community. My father kept all the trophies he had earned in a glass cabinet in the downstairs cellar. He eventually gave up his boxing because of a dodgy knee, not to mention my mother's consistent nagging.

My mother herself was a beautiful woman, with a strong Spanish heritage. She was hired as a nanny and she loved her work. She met my father at a charity dinner hosted by Earl Hampton. The Earl himself was a grand man, he kept within his manor home many antique furniture and souvenirs from his travels, he was a keen huntsman and even though his wife Mildred hated his taste he hung his trophies on the wall as a form of showmanship. Pity the man who would ask him about his African safari days. Once a month, the Earl would host a little get-together. He invited all the local heroes from the area. Thinking about them days made me feel so special to have been the daughter of such special people.

Chapter 3

Riding to the abandoned iron foundry, I could feel the warmth of the wind from the stagnant air. I'm glad I remembered my sunglasses. I had found them on a corpse but, hey he had no further use for them. Wait a minute, what was that? I heard something coming, so I turned my head to see a four-wheeled vehicle pulling over. Oh shit, it's the fucking military again. Pulling over to the side of the road, I climbed off my bike and readily pulled my swords out from behind my leather trench coat. My black leather jeans were a bit ripped, but hey who cares? Here we fucking go again. I spat on the floor. Yeah, I'm no angel... Six big men dressed in black suits, guns at the ready climbed out of a black jeep. They think it's clever to come at me in a group. Big mistake, this will not be pretty.

"Get her men!"

A bald man shouted, and then it starts. Guns are firing at me. Well, they can't kill me, but they still hurt and that's enough to piss me off. Running at them whilst lifting my swords I sliced one vamp at a time. Yes, fucking vamps hanging out with the military. Blood is splattering in profusion; men and vamps are dropping on the road like flies to the curb. Then it happens. A bald man with enormous fists punches me in the face. Well, I didn't see that coming. I fall flat on my arse. Lifting my head, all I could see was a dirty brown sack being put over my head. Oh, shit, as I felt a kick to the head by a fucking boot. Well, this is great. I'm dragged into the armored vehicle and dumped on the seat with my hands handcuffed behind my back.

They lift the brown dirty sack off my head.

"Let's have a fucking look, then. Let's feel how soft her skin feels. And let's have a feel of those beautiful tits, says one of them."

"Why are you smiling, bitch?" says the older man.

"Because I'm going to rip your fucking head off in 30 seconds."

They laughed in disbelief, but it was too late; as I tore the handcuffs apart. Leaning over, I sink my fangs and take a chunk out of the older man's neck. Grabbing a knife from my boot, I fucking stabbed the other man in his head. Blood is squirting out, but do I care? Then I turn to the older man who is now screaming, Grinning, I grab the man's head in my hands, with blood in my mouth. I twist it, hearing the bones snap. I then tear his fucking head off his shoulders and chuck it at the driver. The driver of the vehicle slammed on the brakes. One bloody military man jumps out, and he screams just like a girl

"Bitch, we will have you eventually."

He runs, well when will they learn? I am no angel? I lean in the jeep and pull out the shotgun from the vehicle's back passenger seat. I smirk in a devious way as I aim at the man, watching as the slug travels, giggling as the slug hits the guy in the back of his head, the contents of which splattered everywhere. I was going to let him live. But he got cocky. Knelling on the hard surface of the road, I searched his pockets and I find a card saying "Scablands Industries". I've heard of that name before, but where?

Walking back to my bike, I was thinking about where I'd heard that name before. I know that most companies were owned by the big shots. They've taken over most of the city. I gathered that the factory I'm heading for is owned by them as well.

Arriving, I climbed off my bike. All seemed quiet, so I headed towards the metal shutter doors situated around the back. I attempted to open the door, but of course, it was locked. So I just tore the door open. Heading to the rear of the large factory was where I found large shelves full of multiple boxes. Whilst walking over, I noticed that a few vampires were hanging around in the darkness, watching me. I wondered why they weren't attacking or even shouting at me... Talking of vamps, a few are changing, becoming more independent. A few seem to act differently, it's like someone is controlling them, but how? Before, only a few would listen to commands and be subservient, but they didn't use their minds so to speak. However, latterly they're becoming more self-aware of the environment they are living in, people say some are still just animals and all they want is the blood to control the lust within them.

As night falls, the world is different; they come out of the shadows. They stalk the streets like predators watching their prey. They have been stalking the gun shop lately. I'm sure they are plotting. Only last week I killed a couple of crazy ones. I was collecting a few bits from the market when two shithead vamps tried to jump me, better them dead than me. I've walked the streets many times, noticing the odd vampire eating the remains of a human. So why aren't they attacking? Who fucking knows?

Turning around to grab a box of odds and ends, I hear a man's voice from behind a bunch of crates

"Gloria Snips, is that you?"

Wait, I know that voice, Professor James. He was working on cell theory; I had thought everyone had died in my department. Professor James, the biggest prick in my department. He was caught embezzling money, but it was never proved, he had his so-called lawyer's black mail the judge. What an schmck!

I saw him standing there with a knife in his hand and a gun strapped to his back. He looked well considering, then I noticed he was with the other vamps... He smiled, showing his pointy fangs as if that would threaten me.

"See Gloria, you are not the only one that became an intelligent vamp. But there's one thing you have, and I want your blood. I want to know your bloody secret", He said.

"Fuck you. No one gets to know my secret." Not that I knew it myself.

I drag out my swords and think, here we go again. What the fuck is wrong with these vamps?

"Get her boys!"

The professor sends three vamps at me. One punches me in the face and licking the blood off my lip just excites me. Staring at him, I smiled. With my sword in hand; I sliced off his head. There's a lot of blood, but that's normal. I watched as his body dropped to the floor. The other two come at me. One seems to be a kickboxer. He goes to kick me in the stomach, but I'm faster than him. I throw my sword and it goes through his stomach. Then I punch him in the face and he drops to the floor. Another grabs me from behind. I turn and flip him onto the floor. I pull my sword out of the other's guts and kick him in the head, and two seconds later they both jump up and run off.

"Fucking chickens!" I screamed.

I turn to face the professor, but he's gone. Fuck, his time will come. Riding away from the factory with my blood pumping left me with a shaky feeling. Something more sinister was going on.

Pulling over on the side of the dusty road by the gun shop, I climbed off the bike. I could hear a woman's screams; fuck, it was echoing, from building to building. First, I thought fuck her, it's none of my business, it's just one of the asshole gangs going wild again, but the scream grew louder, more intense. Damn it, I had to go and look, walking over to where the scream was coming from in the next alley.

Knowing this alley had seen many murders, I looked around. Blood was spattered up the walls on either side, resembling crude graffiti. Pulling my swords out, thinking I would need them again, my eyes widened. Something was watching me with its red piercing eyes, and its body was covered with wiry veins. I watched as it crawled around like a cat with a scorpion's barbed tail. What the shit was it? The over-spilled rubbish bins made a clanging sound. Walking I find a young woman; she had short black hair and is wearing a short black skirt and ripped tights. She had a bit of a punk look about her. She must have been about 20ish. She was standing frozen against the wall, sobbing. She was lucky I had turned up. The thing was about to chow down on her for lunch,

"Run!" I said.

Bloody heck what was she doing around this part of the city? This was where the leftover rats and venom lived. It was where I felt most at home. The girl ran off into the night with a rucksack, letting the darkness swallow her. The creature hissed at me. It looked like a wild cat, prowling for its food. It ran at me, and it was fast. I swiped at it with my swords, but I was too slow. The creature hit my swords out of my hands with its tail.

"You little fucker!" I screamed

Pulling out my army-style flick knife from my back pocket I flip it open, I ran at the creature. It was like slow motion. The creature jumped up at me with its fangs dripping with green slime. Lifting my knife, I plunged it at him. I watched as it sliced a piece of its skin from its face; it recoiled in surprise; it acted like a child, screaming and jumping. It whimpered, and a high-pitched sound left its mouth, making me have to cover my ears, with that it ran off into the night.

Picking up my swords, I walked out of the alley to find the young woman sitting on the floor by the gun shop doorway shaking.

"I thought I told you to go."

"I can't. There is nowhere to go. They destroyed my home and killed everyone."

"So, what are you doing here?"

"I was going to Bob's Tool Station when I thought I was being followed."

"What's your name?"

"My name, oh it's Sarah Taylor; I'm an ammunition maker for the military. I worked in the facility before it went nuts. I was making a new weapon called the shock gun. It sends out electrical impulses and renders them unconscious for a few hours. The weapon was in the early stages of its manufacture. I thought I could try to remake it."

Wow, she was innocent. This young girl worked in the same place as me, just in a different department.

"Come on, let's get in."

We walked together, and then went down in the lift, which was old and rickety, but still working. I had found it during my earlier search of the building when I was hunting for supplies. Walking into the gun shop basement, I lit a candle.

"You need genuine power," she said; "I could rig something up for you from the car batteries".

I went to say okay, but she was gone. An hour later, we had power. Most of the electricity in the city had gone out, except for certain parts that ran on private generators. We listened to the radio; I hadn't seen or heard what was happening in other cities in the last two years. A young boy had gotten the word out to the other radio outlets. The virus had spread across the nations; vamps had taken over the world. Fucking great, I thought.

Chapter 4

Sarah had fallen asleep on the bed and was still sleeping when I left the bunker. I knew I needed to find out where the strange-looking scarp (the thing in the alley) came from. Where was it heading back to? I needed to go and investigate, so I went to the alley to pick up the foul smell of the scarp. Squatting down; I pulled my long leather coat from around me and sniffed the air. The air smelt unusually sickling, and somehow strange. But there was a piece of its skin, lying on the dusty ground in the alley; it was where I had sliced a piece of its face-off. I would have to be sure, so I licked it, fucking vamp cross breed, mixed with a hint of a scorpion I would guess. Well, that was new, even for me.

Walking on, smelling the night air, I could see lots of buildings, most of which had been destroyed except for a few blocks which the gangs ran. I followed the scent to the Crown's building it was one of the biggest buildings in the city, how delightful, more to kill. I looked up and noticed a light in the penthouse. It seemed like it would take me ages to reach the top of the staircase. Stopping, I opened the large glass doors and pulled my swords out, just in case.

Screams fall on distant ears. No one cares about the innocents, no one but me. The building was what I expected. Nice polished floors, a large empty desk in front, and a few doors here and there. The lift doors opened and two burly men in black suits, each about 6 feet tall, walked out. Both looked like ex-weight lifters. At first, I thought they were in the military. Well, I thought, until they spoke. Fucking vamps, now that makes sense.

"The boss has been waiting for you."

Their sharp, pointy teeth glimmered as they spoke.

"Hello boys, how's it going?" I said.

They came at me like a pair of bulls in a china shop, their gnarled teeth dripping with slime. I sliced both heads off in one fell swoop, and they dropped to the floor. I hated bloody vamps. I walked past, leaving their corpses to turn to dust. I headed towards the lift. I guess I'm going all the way up. They still had the stupid music playing as I touched the button for the 33rd floor. I reached the top floor. Everything was not what it seemed, it was too quiet. I could see a man standing in front of a burning fire, golden drapes hung from the windows. The man wore a grey suit, probably Italian from the 1930s; he looked about 60 in age.

"I've been waiting for you Gloria; you think I'm stupid?"

"What? And who the hell are you?" I say.

He walks over to me.

"Dearest, don't be nasty, especially with the predicament you are in. You upset my pet; you tore off a piece of his face. Don't you think I deserve an answer?"

He turned around, showing his red eyes glowing, and the arteries in his bald head pulsated. He lifted his hand with his long, pointed fingernails and sent me flying. I hit the wall before landing on a table. Who the fuck is he to do that to me? I bounced back up and I go to strike him. Four of his goons come from behind. I go to kick their asses, but I can't move. It's like a force is keeping me there.

"Get the chains and get that stupid coat off her."

I go to turn and say fuck you, but a punch to the face hits me full on…

Upon waking, I find I'm in a basement area naked. There's a fire blazing. It must be the boiler room. I find I'm chained to a wall and I'm bleeding from the wrists. Fuck, I'm in deep shit. In front of me are the old man and a group of other vamps. At some point, I am sure I saw one of them masturbating whilst grinning at me. He best enjoys himself whilst he can.

"Soon as we get enough of her blood, get it to the facility, hey dork, and stop playing with your fucking dick."

"But boss, look at her, she's hot."

"You can have your fun later," he said, shouting at dork.

"The professor will be there waiting. We don't want to drain her completely, as I need her for my pets need to feed."

Fuck, did he say pets, meaning there's more than one of them ugly fuckers.

I felt weak, trying to pull my chains loose, but I couldn't do it. The old man smiled.

Fuck you, I wanted to say, but I couldn't even talk, I knew they had given me something to keep me sedated. The vamp walked off, leaving my blood to drip in a bowl. Drifting in and out of consciousness, I woke to the sound of a firearm. Instinctively, I lifted my head. I looked up to see a man in his 20s with dark hair, using my swords to part a vamp from his head. I must have drifted back into a stupor because the next thing I knew was the man was carrying me to the lift. Fucking vamps. I looked up at him through my bloody eyes.

"Who are you?"

"I'm your dream man, sweetie. I'm Cables."

Then I passed out again. When I woke up, the lift had stopped at the bottom floor and the doors had opened. There was a car waiting,

"Now get in," he said.

I still felt sleepy climbing into a black sports car as it sped away at high speed.

Chapter 5

I woke up in a small motel room, clumsily dressed. Damn, I thought these places were all burnt out.

"How are you feeling?"

"Just great, apart from a crazy old vamp that has just tried to kill me. What were you doing in the same place as me?" I said.

"Well, it's a long story. The head of the vampire union is my father. When he turned into a vamp, I was a corporal in the military. I stayed human to help the military-run and take back control of the streets. We could control the humans. He would control the vamps. I guess my dad's going to be pissed when he knows I've gone rogue on him. Guess he'll kill me when he finds out I rescued you."

"He's your dad"

"Yeah, I just said didn't I?"

Cables turned to empty his rucksack on the table. He carried a few knives and some extra ammo. The lighting of the room was dim. But I couldn't help but look at him. Damn, he was hot!!

My dinner companion had black short messed-up hair; he had a couple of day's stubble on his rogue chiseled chin. I imagined his fevered body all oiled up with my hands all over him. I hadn't had sex for such a long time, let alone had dinner with a man. I couldn't help myself, I was staring at him. I, the meanest vampire bitch about, I noticed then, that he was smirking,

"So what do we do now sweetie?"

"Don't call me sweetie. My name is Gloria."

"Fair enough sweetie", he giggled.

"So, what's the plan of action?" He said.

"I need to go look at the facility. They are up to something and I need to know what."

"Are you fucking stupid?"

I looked at him and glared. I stood up and headed for the door. He grabbed me by the wrist.

"Let me go, let me go now!"

I was angry. How dare he, I went to pull away and, and he pushed me to the wall!

"You're not going anywhere, sweetie."

Turning, I punched him in the face. I was angry. How dare him! I went to pull away, and he pushed me to the wall again.

Crouching on the floor is a predatory position; diving at him like an animal. I landed on top of him. Then it happened. He kissed me; I felt his warm moist lips touch my stiff lips. No biting, I thought to myself. His tongue was teasing and making me turn into the predatory animal I was. I kept telling myself not to bite; it was so intense. I tore his t-shirt off with my bare hands and my nails sunk into his back. He then pulled my black vest up over my head, pinning me up against the wall, and gripping my necklace, he went to unclasp it.

"No, it stays", I said whilst panting.

Wrapping my legs around him I started to straddle him with my leather jeans on. He smelt different, a sweet but sour smell. Carrying me over to the bed, he tore my trousers off. I then returned the favor. Our naked bodies were entwined, and he hurriedly seized a pair of handcuffs and cuffed me to the bed we were on.

As he spread my legs apart, he kissed me slowly. He kissed his way from my feet up whilst I let out a moan of pleasure. Stopping behind my knees, I found myself gripping the sheets of the bed. I let out a loud moan of pleasure as he licked my pussy with delight. The last time I had sex was so long ago. It was rushed and was just quick shagging, I barely came. I can't even remember the last time someone licked my pussy.

As he slowly moved further up, he used his tongue to explore my body, and as he caressed my breasts with his manly hands, he started to kiss my erect nipples, his teasing tongue tasting me all over. Sending out small electric shocks of pleasure through my body. As he continued to explore my body, kissing my neck, I felt his penis, now hard, brush up against my vagina; his lips continued to kiss my body. He proceeded to enter me slowly, but deliberately, and then his rhythm became more urgent and a little faster. I wanted this so much. I wanted him, even though I felt guilty for some reason. As I let out a moan of delight, he let out a growl, which surprised me but it also made me want him and his dick more. He kept this up for a long time. God was I enjoying this, I've never had a guy be able to thrust inside me for this long before and it was amazing. I let myself feel his muscular body as my arms held him close. I felt my body tense and I enjoyed the best orgasm I can remember, then he kissed me softly and held me tightly while I enjoyed some post-orgasmic bliss.

However, he wasn't done with me yet. After a nice rest, he started thrusting again. I wasn't about to complain. Removing the handcuffs, he turned me over and I gripped the headboard. His dick felt even hotter when he rendered me. He started playing with my anus with a finger. How did he know I enjoyed anal? Then he started to slide his finger in and out of my bum. After he got me loosening up he added a second finger. That was a bit tight and stretched my bum more, but oh it felt good, maybe because I knew what awaited me! Once he was able to slide two fingers up my ass comfortably he pulled out of my pussy. I didn't want him to pull out, but oh did I want him to fill my bum with his dick, and man did he feel me up. Even though he did a good job prepping my anus it still hurt a tiny bit and I let out a small scream. Yes!! I screamed more and more, louder and louder than he pounded me hard!!! This was an out-of-the-world experience. I couldn't believe he could last so long without creaming me. He leaned down to kiss my neck and nibble on my ear, oh was that hot. I felt his body tense along with mine, I turned my head to the sit to bring my mouth to his neck and I bit down on him, hard. He gave a few last hard thrusts as we both came together. I fell flat on the bed and Cables fell on top of me. That one last thrust up my tush was nice. We rolled on our sides, wrapped an arm around me, cupped one of my breasts, and squeezed me tight. We just lay there until his dick finally went limp and fell out of my bum. He rolled on his back and we kissed softly. I lay my head on his chest with a very satisfied look on my face I noticed his bite mark had healed.

"Wow, that was an experience! I've never been with a vampire", he said.

I smirked at him. He propped himself up on his elbow and said.

"Sweetie once is never enough, shall we?"

I giggled like a cheeky schoolgirl and boldly reached for his penis. It didn't take me long to get him hard again. Well, he fingering my bum may have helped a bit.

I rolled on my side again and he came in close behind me. This time his penis just glided through my anus, filling my rectum up again in a big way and we made love again. It was a slower pace and I loved every second of it. Cables gave me a reach around and fingered my vagina and clitoris as he was steadily banging my back door; the combination of stimulations was out of this world. I lost count of how many times I came. I could tell he was getting close as he tensed up, picked up the pace of his thrusting, and drove his cock home as hard as he could each time. One final hard pound against my inside and he moaned loud, sounded kind of like a growl but I was a bit groggy from so many orgasms. We fell asleep rather quickly after that workout. It was wonderful to have him snuggling me close and squeezing me tight as we drifted off to sleep, my anus still stretched around his big cock.

Morning came fast. We both got in the car.

"You can stay at mine. It's not much, but it's safe."

"Cool." he smiled.

We arrived back at the gun shop. Sarah was going crazy. I noticed she had changed into army-colored clothing. She was worried sick. It took her a while to calm down.

"I'm sorry, okay, I was busy."

She looked at me and smirked.

"I've made you something special. It's a vamp net. It cuts them to shreds. I've put it into a gauntlet. You just press that button for it to release. It comes back after it's made the kill."

Was she serious? This was a great idea? I placed it on my arm. I introduced Sarah to Cables, and they both smiled awkwardly at each other.

Sitting on the sofa, we spoke about how it used to be before.

"I need to find a cure, and for that, I need to go to the facility."

Cables looked at me in a frustrated way. What was he trying to cover up? Cables must have his reasons not to want to go, I thought. Or was I just acting suspiciously for no reason?

"Okay, I'm coming then. We will need to get plenty of ammo, and I have the plans to the place in my head"

"I will never forget that place," I said.

"Sarah, you can stay behind."

She felt pleased with that idea, as we both knew it wasn't her cup of tea. I mean, she hated vamps, even though she lived with one.

Showing Cables where I kept my weapons, we grabbed as many hand grenades and firearms as we could carry;

I tied my hair back, and I grabbed a pair of sunglasses. Cables looked at me and laughed.

"We're going full-throttle on the vamps and you wear them?"

I looked at him with a serious look on my face. Let's go. Knowing the facility was huge, most of the building was deep underground. Scientists came from different parts of the world to work on different theories. We had the most up-to-date equipment. The hours were long, but they rewarded us well. When the facility went on lockdown, the army turned up in their vehicles. They targeted the vamps one by one. Before long, the army had taken control with only a few losses. Little did I realize they were joining forces?

When we arrived, the grounds were deserted.

"Over here. There's a secret lift around the back of the facility... Come on, we have to hurry", Cables said.

As we went down in the lift, I couldn't help but wonder what he didn't want to show me.

"Look he said, what the military has been doing had nothing to do with me. What you see down there might make you sick."

I looked at him.

"I'm ready."

As we walked through the corridors, the place seemed different, more advanced.

"Come on, be quiet. We are about to enter the Experimental Department", He said.

We entered the department. I remembered telling Cables the password; he entered it into the keypad.

"Stay to the right, don't get too close to the glass containers, he said"

Cables rambled on about security whilst I walked in front. I couldn't help myself. The military was working on something. Peering into the glass container, something glared back at me. It was a young girl about 8 years old. She looked innocent. Then it happened. The girl camouflaged herself in the background of the glass container.

"What the fuck was that? I said.

"She's a vamp crossed with a chameleon. She can change her skin to match her background. It tells you on the wall over there where it says specimen one."

As we walked on, I couldn't help but think about putting her out of her misery. We then came across another room. I peeped in there and what I saw blew my mind. There was a food bank, a fucking slaughterhouse id call it, with hundreds of humans just hanging up. They had pipes connected to them and were being drained of their blood. This was barbaric. I know I was a vamp, but it was so wrong on so many levels. My gut said to kill everyone and everything. Most were dying anyway. Looking in the room cables said,

"Fuck them, poor people"

"Should I kill them? I can put them out of their misery."

"No wait, let's carry on looking. There has to be some kind of paperwork, from the first initial experiments; I guess they will be in the main lab on the upper floor."

Cables walked in front and I thought to myself, fuck it. I pulled out my swords and sliced the bags open, and their liquid contents spilled onto the floor. I then switched off all the machines that were keeping the bodies alive. The red alarm goes off.

"Cables, I'm going to stay and fight," I said.

"Damn it, I fucking knew it. Looks like I'm staying too then."

We both waited. We noticed the doors shut, the whole goddamn facility was closing down. I chucked a hand grenade and within a second, an enormous explosion took the doors out. We made our move. Shame, the military and a group of vamps were waiting for us on the other side.

"We can either run or fight," Cables said.

Looking at him and smiling. I ran at them, two military men fired at me. The bullets stung, but I didn't give a shit. I struck one man with a blow to his face. He went down. Cables were fighting one of the military men in a menacing battle. Blow for blow, he impressed me. He had spunk. Raising my swords, I went after the vamp. I was about to use my swords again, but something from behind me took my legs out. I went down; I stood up and looked about, but there was nothing. Then I heard a scream. One of the military men was lying on the floor screaming. I looked down to see the little girl from the container. She smiled at me as she fed.

"Come on Gloria; let's get the fuck out of here! We can't fight them all. This way, he shouted!"

Scampering up the stairs leading to the roof, as I turned to look back I saw that the little girl had let the other experiments out of their containers. I turned to see them fighting. Taking the other vamps out, I was running behind Cables when something caught my legs and I went down. Getting back up, I noticed there was that nasty-looking scarp from the alley. I looked even closer at it. This one was different, and it was twice as large. My legs were hurting from the sting the tail had inflicted upon me. I must have not noticed before, as my adrenaline was pumping. Then I saw Cable's Father. Hearing footsteps coming from behind, I turned to see Cables being escorted by three vamp security guards...

I rode back with tears running down my face. My leg had healed by itself. I guess I liked that part about being a vampire. Worrying about Cables, I returned home. I was hurt, but I had a job to do. Standing in the rickety lift, it went down; I opened the door to find Sarah deep in car parts.

"Where're cables to?"

She said as I sat down on the sofa. I told her the whole story. She looked surprised but understood. Taking my boots off and laying on the sofa, I pulled a blanket over me. What a fucking day. With that, I passed out. Morning came quickly; I was awoken by someone banging the fuck out of my door,

"Okay, I'm coming"

I made sure I had a knife on me, just in case. Fuck. Who was knocking on my door? No one knew I was here, except...

"Cables, what the fuck? I thought you were dead"

"My dad was sleeping, so I stole his car keys, she a beaut as well. I think you need this"

He passed me back my coat. He walked in as if he didn't care about the world.

"So tell me, what happened after he took you in the car?

"Well, I told him I saw another vamp letting you free, I said that you forced me, and threatened to rip my balls off if I didn't help you, he was slightly concerned but he knows I'm a big boy."

Fucking great, I thought, more shit to deal with. We both walked in and sat down. I grabbed the papers which we had taken from the lab and started to go through them, to look for anything that made sense. Nothing at all looked normal until I notice an envelope that was stapled to the papers.

"What that you got there?" said Cables.

Opening it, I started to read, it was a quick note with directions to a cave.

"What the fuck is going on?" I said.

"I think it's a clue to the hidden element of the drug. It says in the notes that they had found a cave which contained a special ingredient, but it didn't say what."

"The plot thickens", Sarah said giggling.

"Yes, it does for sure."

Sarah pieced together that road trips were a bad trigger to my past life. I and my father would go on father-daughter trips to the great outdoors. It was dad's way of getting a weekend off from my mother's nagging. We visited Matlock Lakes, where the waters were calm; we stayed in a log cabin which my dad built with his own hands. I wonder if it's still there. Cables were looking at the directions on the piece of paper. Whilst I started to pack, Sarah was rushing around, grabbing her essential supplies. I walked over to the fridge. Since we had the power, I had filled the bottom shelf with pockets of animal blood. I grabbed a handful and put them into a green army rucksack. With a few odds and ends, i.e. torches, a couple of knives, and the usual stuff.

"Looks like we're using the car then," said Cables.

Walking to the lift, I couldn't help but think about what we would find. The cave was deep in the mountains and we had to be prepared for whatever the outcome was. Putting our stuff in the boot, Sarah climbed in the back seat. Looking at Cables; I noticed he had a grin on his face.

"What's with the stupid smile?"

"Oh nothing, I was just thinking about my dad, he's so going to kill me."

I was thinking he was a daddy's boy. We drove through the town without a word. I had taken to looking at the handwritten directions. It took us to the east of Peak Canyon Mountains, shit I thought, I hate that place. I thought something was watching me as we drove down the road.

We had gone there camping as teenagers. I was 18, and one night I and a small group of friends got drunk on spirits. I had decided to wobble off for a pee with only a torch for light and I thought I heard a rustle in the bushes. I remembered looking but only the sound of the owls could be heard. I walked back to the campsite and crawled into my tent, nervously I tried to sleep. But I wasn't alone. Someone or something was stroking my face with its hand. I felt the touch of another hand feel my thigh and move slowly up my skirt. I was frozen in fear as the light pressure against my leg slowly moved towards my thigh and also slowly slid to the inside of my thigh. I had never been touched like this before. I was scared, excited, horny, and intrigued. I lay perfectly still, like a statue, part out of fear and part out of curiosity. I wanted to see how close the light reassure would get to my pussy and more importantly how it would feel. I had fingered myself loads of times, but no one else had ever touched my body in this way and I was down for finding out how it would feel. I heard the loudest owl screech and I jumped up scared. I looked quickly, but there was no one there. I don't know who, or what had been touching me so sensuously but it was gone now. I had put what had happened to me to the back of my mind till now. I shuddered. Sarah looked at me in a puzzled way; I gave her a quick smile before sinking myself deeper into the black leather seat of the car. Sitting next to Cables made me feel excited. I wanted to pull over and send Sarah for a walk so I could jump his bones; I think he guessed as he moved his hand onto my thigh. Sarah kept looking at me with a devilish look in her eye.

"What Sarah?"

"Just come out with it."

"Okay, why are you able to walk in daylight? You're still human in so many ways."

I stared at her for a while before saying,

"I don't know."

I noticed it from the very start. I was cleaning up and my hand slipped into the light. I was expecting an awful burn, but nothing, I didn't even sizzle. So I walked outside and still nothing. I knew then I was a Daywalker.

"I thought they were none existent. I mean, I had read them in fiction books but never did I think they were real Sarah"

"Damn Gloria, you are a rarity. Imagine if the other fangs knew."

Sarah raved on and on until we reached the rocks. Cables drove without saying a word.

Chapter 6

The cave was about halfway up the canyon and we knew night-time was falling upon us so we built a campfire. Sarah with her blanket and her bag under her head slipped into a deep sleep. Cables gathered more firewood for the night. I could have, and should have, fucked him as I wanted to ravish his muscular body, but I had a fear of dread, that took me away to my old camping trip.

Taken to doing nothing, I walked to where I stayed as a teen. I mean, it couldn't hurt me; I was a mean bitch of a vamp now. I gulped. I looked for the tree we had all sung and laughed together around. I had a habit of that, singing when I was drunk. After a while, I found it and touched the old oak with its rough bark. It brought back an array of emotions. Not just good ones either. My stomach churned. I focused on something different. The smell in the night air took me miles away to where a party of vamps was hanging out, drinking and dancing around a huge fire while some revved the engines of their bikes in delight. Sitting there for a moment I ran my hand across the initials, thinking then I smelt it, someone else was with me here, another vamp's essence, but they were a lot older, maybe even hundreds of years old. I turned with my sword in hand, but there was no one, only a fox running past. I told myself I was overreacting to the situation. I went to walk away but something pushed me onto the cold, damp moist ground. My swords landed on the wet ground beside me. Feeling frozen, my eyes darted through the darkness, laying there, I clenched the grass as I felt someone's hands travel up my vest and feel my bare breasts; I felt its kiss touch my lips and move down my body, whilst its hands pulled my trousers down and took my shoes off, I was being raped by an invisible force. I couldn't move, I was immobilized to the ground. The force lifted me in the air as it pulled my legs apart I felt it enter me. By then I had started to pant intensely as it bared itself down on me, pushing it harder and harder between my groins. I let out a moan in delight, and I felt its lips touch mine again as it moved to my neck and started to bite it. I was being raped. Part of my mind was saying this is a bad situation, but part of my mind was enjoying it and wanting more. What was this invisible force that was giving me so much pleasure and pain all at once?

"Gloria!"

I heard cables shout out. I went to shout, but I was still naked. I didn't want him to see me. I didn't want to say something really weird had happened; he would think I'm damn right crazy. The presence had let me free. I quickly put my clothes back on and headed to the campsite. I didn't look back.

"Gloria, I was worried about you. Where the heck have you been?"

I proceeded to tell him about the tree. Sitting around the campfire made me feel warm; Cables wrapped his arms around me and gave me a sweet kiss.

"Your mine."

I heard a voice whisper in my ear

"Remember who you are."

Feeling startled I tried to shake the voice off by kissing Cables again.

The voice whispered again. I ignored it and sat there quietly, waiting for the sun to rise. Noticing Cables' hands had been bleeding. I lifted his hand and sucked his knuckles.

"Next time I'll be more careful picking up wood", He said, smiling.

He didn't think I noticed the look in his eyes. The look of fear and anger didn't go unnoticed.

Did he know? Did he see?

Cables' pov

Picking up wood from the forest, I couldn't help but think about what was in the cave. Did I want to know my dad's full operation? I knew I had to get that thought out of my head, so I imagined fucking Gloria. Feeling randy, I thought I would wander back to the camp and make love to my sweet Gloria, but she was amiss. I went hunting for her. I searched the darkness of the forest and I found Gloria. What I saw made me hide behind a tree and punch it several times. All I could do was to watch, feeling angrier and angrier, something dark was fucking my girl, an invisible force, and worse still she looked to be enjoying it. I felt like yelling and going nuts but I watched as she tried to struggle but something was forcing her, but whom, I watched as her body lifted into the air and her legs were spread apart and something was making her moan All I could do was to pretend to be looking for her as I watched her body float up and down, I couldn't help it I ran out from behind the tree yelling Gloria where are you, I watched with fear in my eyes, as she floated naked back down to the ground. It got me thinking uncomfortable thoughts. Did I satisfy her enough, or was this terror of the night better than me in the sack, damn I was so fucking angry. Something raped my girl. My knuckles bled again, so I licked up the blood, it was not to be seen running down my hands. I slowly made my way back to the camp with so many emotions I nearly puked.

Gloria's Pov

When the morning arrived, the sun was blazing down on the tranquil forest, leaving a beautiful shimmering effect coming off the fresh green leaves. Looking around and taking in the scenery I felt a peaceful feeling like I belonged here, it felt so different from last night. I sniffed at the warmth of the air and let my senses drift me away for a brief moment, I could smell the morning dew of springtime in the air, and I focused hard and zoomed in on the flowers opening up their petals whilst the bees danced around their beautiful petals. Sarah was just waking up whilst Cables made some coffee. I sneaked off to drink my morning glory of fresh coffee. Standing by a tree, I sipped at my coffee whilst looking up at the caves. I thought what if?

Cables walked over and kissed me softly and I noticed something unusual: his knuckles were healed. I was getting suspicious. If he was a Daywalker like me, why did he hide it and what other things was he keeping from me? Looking up, I realized that Sarah couldn't climb great enormous boulders of rock. I found myself staring at her.

"What, she said."

"I may have to carry you upon my back when we climb."

"Like cheese nibbles, are you? I'll walk"

"Oh come on Sarah, stop being a pain", I giggled.

"Okay, we'll find another way"

She ran over and wrapped her arms around me.

Cables turned around, "Come on, and let's go!" he said.

Walking in the heat didn't bother me, but Sarah looked like she was about to drop. We had only walked 5 miles through the rocky terrain.

"I need to rest." Sarah cried out.

"I just can't do it. How's about I set up camp and you pair go-ahead?"

"Okay", I said after a while.

I handed her a gun and some spare ammo in case the shit hit the fan, so to speak. Cables and I helped her set camp. Leaving her alone made me feel awkward, but she begged me.

Cables were particularly quiet, so I asked him straight out:

"You saw, didn't you?"

"Yeah, what the fuck was that? I watched it rip your damn clothes off Gloria. I felt fucking useless. You're my gal, and something raped you, and all I could do was watch. I feel fucking ashamed of myself "

Walking over to him, I wrapped my arms around him, thinking whether I should ask him whether he was like me, or should I wait.

"If I ever find out what it was, I'll tear it apart with my bare teeth."

Okay, honey calm down, I'm a big girl I'll deal with it.
"

It was then I noticed it a gap in the rocks, maybe even a way up.

"Look over there."

Before heading for the gap, I needed to drink.

"Pass me some blood from my bag."

I watched Cables very carefully as he passed me my drink, to see if he showed a lust for the blood, nothing not a bloody thing. After drinking, I licked my lips. The taste was amazing.

Heading through the gap, we came to a tunnel. It looked like an old mining tunnel. They must have used it to excavate rocks, or they were digging for gold. Either way, it was abandoned. As I walked through the darkness, I grabbed Cable's hand tightly. Even though I was a vamp, I found this place spooky and looking ahead, I heard Cables shout:

"Something is over here!"

I froze. Whose hand was I holding if it wasn't Cable's? I slowly gripped my knife and went to stab the thing next to me, but there was no one there. I felt a cold wind pass me and a male's voice saying,

"Come to me, my wife."

I walked up to Cables and grabbed him. I couldn't stop but hold him tightly in my arms. I started to sob.

"What's wrong Gloria?"

"We're not alone. There's someone with us in this tunnel"

Cables gripped his gun. This was the first time since that camping trip I'd been scared. We lit my lighter to look at what it was. It looked like an old part of the tunnel, but someone had used wood and nails to cover the entrance. We looked closer and written in Latin were the words "cave intret tu peticula".

"What's that mean?" Cables said.

"It means beware, enter at your own risk."

Cables went to leave, but a voice was saying:

"Gloria, my love, please come to me."

The voice egged me on and a part of me wanted it. I tore the wood apart piece by piece with my bare hands.

"Cables help"

"Gloria let's just leave it, this place is damned, there could be anything down there."

Cables grabbed my hand and went to pull me away.

But something picked him up and flung him in the air. I watched as he recklessly bounced off the rooks and hit the ground with a loud thud. Cables shot up, but he wasn't my fun-loving Cables anymore. He let out a humongous growl that echoed down the tunnel. Upon turning, I watched as he tore his clothes off into a mass of shreds. His hands changed to massive paws and long, sharp claws grew. I watched as he morphed into an 8-foot tall bear weighing over 8oo pounds. He was ferocious! He looked at me as if to say, I'm sorry, my love. Well, blow me. I thought he was a vamp or a werewolf, but a fucking bear. I watched as the bear ran at the invisible force and I'm sure I saw a man's figure 6 foot tall, dark-haired, tattoos traveling up his arms fucking good looking too; I watched them both fight in mortal combat blow for blow. My boyfriend looked to be winning at one point. Blood was dripping from Cables. His front leg was a wrangled mess. Then it happened. The man jumped onto cables back and I watched in horror as he snapped my boyfriend's neck. I let out a scream that bounced off the rock walls. Sobbing I ran to Cables, he'd already transformed back to human, if you will. Cradling Cables in my arms, I knew what had to be done... I knew he could heal himself, but not from death itself.

Sobbing and scanning for the man who killed my beloved, I bite down on Cables' neck and damn well hoped he could come back. Sitting there in the dark of the tunnel waiting, I felt a hand stroke my face. I knew that sensation and I had for hundreds of years. The man picked me up in his arms as he carried me down the tunnel. I drifted into his dreamy brown eyes.

Chapter 7

Sarah's POV

Sitting on the grass cuddled by the warmth of the fire with my coffee cup in one hand and my soft grey blanket wrapped around me, I looked up at the blanket of stars. I was worried sick. What if something bad had taken place in the tunnels? What if… Something startled me to the point I was distracted from my train of thought. It was coming from the bushes behind me. I dropped my coffee mug and slowly picked up a stick from the pile of wood. I proceeded to head towards where the noise was coming from. The bushes rustled as I came closer to the noise.

"Who's there?"

Nothing, I started to panic, but then I noticed a rabbit came running out. I started to cry. I was so damn scared and oh did I have to pee. I got a good footing, loosened my britches, and squatted down. Oh, did it feel good to pee; I guess I had to go. As I kept peeing I had this nagging feeling something was watching me. Eh, I'm not going to worry about a cute little bunny, even if he did startle me. I felt much better walking back to camp with an empty bladder, I guess I drank more coffee than I thought. I sat down, touched my watch, and sent out a homing signal. I'm sure my friends would come.

"Sarah, what's up, is everything going to plan?"

"Yes, but she's not alone sir, Cables is with her and she taking ages to get back. What shall I do?"

"Make your way to the tunnels, we'll meet you."

"Okay, stay safe."

Cables' Blood Lust

Watching from a tree, I couldn't help but dribble onto my bare skin. Her flesh was egging me to feast, in more ways than one. Hooking up with Gloria was amazing but Sarah is quite the little hottie herself. Seeing her bare bum got me thinking about Gloria, and hard. It was then I saw a rabbit run from a nearby bush. Gripping it with my hands; I broke its neck. I tore a chunk out of its neck and ate the rest. I was still starving. I needed more. The blood lust was driving me insane, but I felt like if I was to feast on a human, I would become a full bear with no control. What the heck was wrong with me? I remember waking up in the tunnel alone, and all I could think about was the taste of food. Realizing my senses had taken over; I wandered off, out of the tunnel and sniffed the sweat air. There was somebody close. Climbing down the rock cliffs I noticed this girl. I licked my lips. I watched as she drank what looked like coffee by the fire. Moving out from behind a tree, I felt a hard whack across the back of my head, and all I can see as I hit the ground is an outline of what looked like a man. Waking up, I found myself only wearing a pair of ripped jeans and no top. I was chained to a wall. I tried to pull at the chains,

"Son you couldn't leave it alone. You had to go meddle. I also see someone has messed with you and now I have a vamp bear for a son"

I looked up, and for a brief moment, I saw a woman's face saying:

"Cables help!"

Gloria, shit. I needed to get out of here and get back to the tunnel.

"Bring him some food."

My father said as he left the room. The vamp dragged a young girl in. She must have been about 20. She was on some sort of drug that made her docile; the vamp used his nails to cut the girl's wrist.

"Here, eat."

I knew then if I was to eat her, I would lose myself, and that was when I flipped. I felt the change taking place. I was more than a bear. I was a werebear. I tore the chains from the wall and gripped the girl and chucked her to the ground.

"Stay!"

I said, growling. She was now sobbing into her hands.

Pouncing on the vamp, I tore them apart piece by piece, feasting on his lovely flesh and blood. My blood lust was over. Shit, I thought I knew what I was, and I was going to eat. Sarah and I would have lost full control. Running through the doors at full force, I ripped them apart. Men were using weapons against me. Fuck, I knew then I was in the facility again. All I could do was worry about Gloria.

Gloria's pov

Waking up on a glorious wooden carved four-poster bed with a white sheet draped over my body took me by surprise; I'd expected to still be in the tunnel. Looking at my surroundings, I took in all the details. The walls were patterned in beautiful yellow flowers, and my bedding was made of Egyptian white cotton, at the end of my bed against the wall was a white dressing table. Listening I could hear a lovely piano being played, the music was ancient-fashioned but beautiful. Climbing out of bed I glanced over to see my reflection in the mirror on the dressing table, it was me but not me my hair was longer, and curls bounced down my naked bosom. Walking over to the long windows, I looked out. Seeing a beautiful lawn with its 18th-century statues on the ground with a pond was in the middle, I'm guessing it contained freshwater goldfish as I stood there I kept thinking, was I imagining things, this life was so perfect down to the painted statues? Turning back around, I couldn't believe it. There was a beautiful red satin gown placed on an elegant yellow chaise lounge. Slipping it on, I looked at myself as I brushed my hair with an antique, silver hairbrush. Heading back down the long, beautiful carved staircase, which twisted and turned me, I looked at the walls to see myself and the man that killed my beloved, with his arms wrapped around me. Freezing, I couldn't help but admire the picture with the gold frame. The idea of being married to this man shocked me but excited me to the core. Taking deep breaths, I carried on walking. Was I crazy or was I feeling damn Horney?

"Gloria, my darling, have some breakfast", a man spoke.

As I walked into the grand room, a fire was burning away in the grate. Piping hot food was placed on a white tablecloth on a long wooden table; a very handsome man with black hair and puppy dog eyes approached me and kissed me on the lips.

"My darling, how did you sleep?"

I stuttered before saying,

"I slept fine"

Oh god, he tasted divine on his soft moist lips that brought a little smile to my lips. Noticing him smiling, I sat down on the wooden chair.

"Darling, after breakfast, we should pack our belongings. The ship will be leaving tonight at 9 pm."

I smiled while I ate what looked like eggs benedict. I noticed the way he watched me seducing me with every inch of his eyes, yet I still couldn't remember our life together. After finishing my breakfast I made my way up the staircase and back to my room, where a claw foot tub full of warm steamy water was waiting for me. Turning to see the Count, I put my head down, but he lifted my chin with his soft warm hands and kissed me, oh the lovely taste of his lips. He slowly undressed me, piece by piece and I let him. As I climbed into the bath he grabbed a sponge and put some soap on it, gently he washed me, not saying a word. Standing up, he dried me off. Touching my lips with his fingers, he kissed my neck gently. Lifting me and carrying my naked body to the bed was such a nice end to being bathed, he placed me down gently. Softly and slowly, he caressed my ample breasts with his hands before moving himself lower. Using his moist lips and tongue, he licked my pussy. I started to moan uncontrollably and climaxed a dozen times. After a couple of hours of his fingers gently playing with my pussy and bum while he licked my clit, he inserted his hard cock deep into my pussy, which was now dripping. He settled into me with wonderful rhythm and motions, he pumped over and over till we both climaxed together.

Memories from long ago came flooding back to me, memories from our past life together. I was indeed Countess Dracula.

Within an hour, after lying wrapped up in Vals' arms, I heard a young boy's voice shouting:

"Mother, I'm home from school!"

Hector was 11 and looked just like his father with his beautiful brown eyes. He was nothing more than pleasant. Running into our bedroom, he dived at us both. He looked at me and wrapped his arms around me.

"I love you mummy"

"Go on downstairs. Lucy will be there" Val said.

Lucy was the maid, but she spent her time keeping Hector Company during the holidays. Getting dressed, I watched as they played tag on the lawn. I didn't want this feeling to end.

"Wait Gloria, I have a gift for you before we go downstairs."

He passed me a box and opened it up. I grinned and kissed him sweetly. There was a ruby stone set in a gold ring with a matching necklace. He placed it on me, kissed me, and then slapped my rump. We spent the rest of the day laughing and dancing to fine music.

"Gloria, I have to go to the docks. I've had a delivery. Do you and Hector fancy a ride in the carriage?"

That morning, we dressed in our finest of clothes, ready for the ride out of town. Looking back at the many windows and the grand lawn, I smiled briefly; I was happy. Hector was wearing his brown waistcoat over his white shirt, his brown breeches, and white stockings with his best shoes.

"Come on, let's go."

Riding away in the carriage was the last time we were all together.

Memories can be painful reminders that leave us with revengeful thoughts.

Reaching the docks took most of the day. It had gotten dark and started to rain. Val was looking for a man he was meant to meet to collect his shipment of fine fur coats. Hector and I stood against a wall waiting whilst Val went to meet him.

A group of men was watching me intently and one of them, dressed in a stripped grey suit, started to follow my husband. Suddenly Hector let go of my hand, sprinted, and yelled,

"Father!"

I watched in horror as the man following my husband pulled out a knife; he was aiming for Val but our son lunged in the way. Watching Hector fall to the ground I let out a scream that echoed through the docks. I cried as I ran to Hector. I saw my husband sitting there holding our son. Val's hands were covered with our son's blood; Hector's was the palest white I've ever seen.

Val could barely speak. "He's gone love, I couldn't stop the bleeding." I let out a scream that echoes across the docks.

"Where is he?"

The police searched high and low but the man was gone, they left Hector's case open.

Revenge can change a man.

Two weeks later, after Hector's burial, Val took to the streets hunting for the man that killed our boy. All I could do was lie there in pain. The doctor said it was TB. Soon word got out and Val returned home.

Val's pov

Watching as my son died in my arms broke my heart as though it had been snapped into a million pieces and scattered across the universe. I couldn't face Gloria after the funeral. I panicked, even though I wanted to hold her so badly. Yet I was a total mess. Leaving Gloria and the home my son played in felt like some sort of release, yet the terrors of that perused me, I went from house to house but nothing, no one knew of him. Walking into a tavern wasn't one of my brightest ideas. I inspected around all walks of life and visited here old sailors with tales to tell, and girls with low-cut tops offering services for drinks. Thieves, highwaymen, smugglers, and sailors waiting for ships. Tankards were full of beer, rum having been smuggled in from far places. Sitting down, feeling miserable and a full-on coward, I ordered a beer. The girl smiled at me as she flashed her breasts.

"Here is your drink lovely"

I took it and thanked her.

Looking around, I could see a man coming toward me.

"We've been looking for you for some time sir; I have an urgent telegram for you."

I took the letter and thanked the gentleman. Reading the letter, I sunk deeper into my seat. My Gloria, the love of my life, was dying, and the thought was devastating. She had TB, and it was going to take her away from me. I couldn't stand the thought. I had already lost our only son. I sat in my seat watching the fire burn in the grate and the flames danced to the sound of old folk music. An old stranger approached me wearing a fine black suit with a black cloak and a wooden walking stick.

"May I be of service?"

He said as he sat down, I'd like to help you with your problem, I have this bottle it, contains a potion for eternal life but it comes with a heavy price tag. If you drink it you can live forever and can wait for your wife to become reborn.

"What the catch?"

"You will become a creature of the night and you will need to feed on human blood"

He said, smiling at me. His eyes had a hint of reddish. He must have been very sick, or he was on opium.

"Drink it, it will bring you the power and strength my boy to live forever".

"Did you say I'll crave for?"

"Blood my boy, blood. You see boy, if you live forever you'll be there for when Gloria is reborn."

I went to ask how much, but the man was gone and the small bottle was left on the table. I put the small bottle in my pocket and carried on drinking. I was rather drunk upon leaving the tavern. I went to go see Gloria. On my way back to the carriage, the small bottle in my pocket was teasing me to drink. It whispered,

"Drink me, I am yours."

I climbed into the carriage and pulled the curtains closed. Pulling out the small bottle, I looked at it closely. Forever is a long time but I will see my Gloria again, so for that, it's worth it?

"Bottoms up," I said as I drank it.

It tasted like death itself. As it hit my stomach I felt myself die from within. My insides were burning like a fire that had gone wild in a forest. Heat traveled up my skin as I watched myself burn alive. Upon waking up, I had a desperate need for food and was not of the usual type. The old driver of the cartridge was good, but sometimes a little clumsy. As he rode at the front of the cartridge, he was fiddling with his pocket knife and accidentally cut himself.

"Damn it!"

The man carried on driving like it was nothing until he noticed something climbing on the roof of the cartridge.

I couldn't help myself. The smell was seducing me and I was starving. Slowly climbing out of the cartridge and onto the roof I was about to tear him apart, but Gloria's beautiful face appeared in front of me. I pounced off the carriage and ran away into the darkness of the night. I couldn't bear the thought of being a creature of the night. I traveled to the cemetery, sat at my son's grave, and cried. I begged God to bring him back, not just for me, but for Gloria too. I stayed there for two nights not eating. Heading back home, I felt weak and sick, but I needed to see my wife.

Gloria pov

As I lay there in the darkness of my room with the breeze coming through my opened window, I sensed Val was with me.

"You came back," I said in a weakened voice.

"My darling, you cannot see me like this," he said in a strange tone.

"Darling, I have seen you in every way. Please tell me what has happened"

With that, Val broke down and told me everything.

"Val, please lift me onto my pillow more.

Mine and Val's love were true from the very moment we meet. We were destined to be together forever. Val sat on the end of my bed and told of his desperation and sadness. Weeping, I softly spoke to Val. "It's your choice, but I would like to die knowing that you will not starve."

"Val, let me be your first taste. Take all that I am till we meet again." He sobbed.

"I'll wait till you are reborn. I promise we'll meet again, I love you so much."

With that, he sunk his teeth into me, and I died in his arms.

Val's pov

Holding her in my arms, I couldn't help but cry. She was so beautiful, her long black locks flowed down her body; I wanted her to be alive, but I know I had sucked too much of her blood. Placing her body back down on her bed. I kissed her and said.

"Till I meet again my love."

Taking her jewelry, I knew I had to keep it safe till my Gloria was reborn. I would wait in the shadows, feed on the animals, and travel the globe till the time was right.

180 years later

I needed to set the scene for her to find the necklace; for I knew what was to come in the new world. Being this old has its insights. I considered just handing it to her, but it had to be more of a surprise. So I broke into her bedroom whilst her parents were away, knowing Gloria would return for spring break. You see I had watched her grow up; I visited whilst she slept so no harm would come to her, knowing she would turn 18. I needed to hide the necklace. Placing it in an old box, I kissed it before hiding it.

I knew she was the one from her scent; I picked up her pillow and smelt it. You see, my wife gives off a pleasant smell of moonflowers; she kept these in our garden back in 1845 and used them as a perfume. It's a smell of lavender and a hint of white roses. Gloria placed the flowers on Hector's grave.

Visiting her room often, I knew she had been offered a placement in a high-tech facility. It had been used as a nuclear experimental facility in the 1940s. I had the memories to prove it, but that was another lifetime. Looking around her room, I picked up her pillow with the white frills and sniffed her scent again. I missed her so much. Visiting her whilst she slept is the only way at present to see her. So I send her my love and tell her she's amazing. We have a connection; call it eternal love or a mental bond. Making love to her in her dreams was all that we had. Picking up her diary, I sat down to read.

Gloria's diary

Monday 12th, 2014

It's been an unusual week, been having these dreams, keep seeing a man's face, but it fades and I'm left in tears upon waking. It feels like I've known him for years. Yesterday I got invited to go camping for the weekend near the canyon, there's a swimming lake near there so hope I get to use it.

Tuesday 13th, 2015

Can you be in love with someone from your dreams? Every moment I see him, my whole body feels alive?

Wednesday 14th

Packing for the camping trip today

Placing the book down, I knew I had to see her, plus I was so damn Horney, but I couldn't let her see me, not just yet. I didn't want to scare her, not before she remembered me.

Chapter 8

Sarah's pov

I couldn't understand where they had got to. Night-time would soon be here and I needed to find them. Packing up my belonging and putting the fire out, I made my way. I needed to get to the caves and was in a hurry, but I had a feeling it was going to take me a while. The path was treacherous, and I knew I could die. Gloria, Cables! I yelled, nothing, just the warm breeze. Looking up at the cave, I couldn't help but have an uncomfortable feeling that something scarier than a vampire lived there. Sitting for a while, I saw three black 4x4 vehicles turning up. Each has at least 6 men in.

"Shit!"

I thought, grabbing my gun I heard a voice say "Sarah, we're coming up the other side of the path, will be with you in five". I felt guilty for not telling Gloria I was part of an ancient association called the Brotherhood of Truth that had been following Dracula for hundreds of years. We had followed him ever since the 18th century, being a legacy it was my duty to make friends with and to follow the wife of the count. We'd just been routinely compiling information, keeping parchments of individual sightings from around the world, till we came upon a painting of Dracula and his wife, the painting was stolen and sold on the black market a week later.

Cables pov

Ripping three vamps apart with my bare hands made me feel inevitable, yet the thought of Gloria drove me on

"Stop!"

Shouted my father

"I need you to see something."

Turning around, I spat out the last of the vamp from my mouth. I looked at my father.

"What can you possibly want to show me?"

"it's about Gloria, you don't think I've had my men watch her for the past year for no reason, I didn't just want her blood, I needed to find out where she came from and if what I had seen about her was right"

"What do you mean by saw?"

"Here, follow me."

My father said, walking towards the lift.

"I didn't want you to get hurt, not by this"

"You chained me up, father"

"I did it for your damn safety."

We walked to the lift, and he pressed the button for the basement. Reaching the bottom had left me with a feeling of bitterness. We carried on walking through the basement, where the fire in the furnace fuelled the place, till we came to a door that was hidden away behind an old wooden bookcase.

"This is where I keep the artifacts and my expensive art from the museums".

He walked over to a canvas that was covered in an old dust cloth and pulled it away. Looking at the canvas blew my mind. There was this painting dated back to the 18th century. The picture had been hand-painted. It showed a beautiful woman in a red satin dress with a handsome man with his arms wrapped around her. Fuck I stood back in shock or was it disbelief. The woman was my Gloria. Upon looking closer at the painting I saw a little written message saying "Gloria my wife may our love last forever. Yours, Count Val Dracula". Falling to my knees in despair I sobbed. Looking at my dad, I spoke in a weakened voice.

"Why take her blood, why chase her?"

"Dracula, that's why. She's the key to eternal life. Boy, her blood tells a story that's been around for hundreds of years. Son, she's the wife the Dracula himself."

"I don't bloody care. I love her and I'm sure she loves me"

Well, that's what I told him. Seriously, what the fuck? I was devastated.

Walking away, I told my father I'm going home, when in fact I was going to the gun shop to tool up.

Chapter 9

Present-day, Gloria's pov

Waking up in the tunnel with Val Dracula by my side, I felt suddenly safe. He looked at me and smiled. I had read somewhere that true love lasts millions of years, no matter where you are in the universe.

"I see you're wearing the necklace I gave you."

"Yes, I found it when I was 16 in an old shoebox. I've always worn it."

"Yes, my love, it's a sunstone, it's special. It lets you walk in the daylight. There's only one of its kind, and you have it."

What now? I was about to say it when I heard a voice behind me say.

"Get your stinking hands off my fucking girl"

Turning around, I looked in Cables' direction.

"Stop Cables, Don't! Please, you don't understand"

"Gloria, I've come back to rescue you, that thing fucking snapped my neck!"

I growled at him "He's my husband, I love him!"

With that, I heard something

"Quiet, someone's coming"

I licked my lips and grabbed my swords, which were leaning up against the tunnel wall. Smiling at Val and then at Cables.

"Let's play boys."

The tunnels were long and wiry; the dirty, stagnant air left the tunnels with a cold feeling. The smell of humans made me want to feed intensely, I considered I must have been starving. With that I watched in silence as two, 6-foot men in their late thirties, all in black walked towards us.

"They're mine," I said.

Val grinned.

"I'll take the next two. I need to let some anger out."

Cables said as he stared at Val.

Smiling, I ran towards the men. Both swords in my hand, I fucking hated the military, and worse still; they were working with Cables' father. Slicing one man in the stomach with my sword made me smile. Blood gushed out, leaving the man clutching himself. The other man shot at me.

"Don't worry. I got this Hun."

Val yelled as he dragged the other man down the tunnel screaming; the smell of blood was calling me so bad, I dribbled and then I heard Cables shout.

"Don't Gloria! It will change you; you'll be just like him."

With that, I sank my teeth into the man's neck.

As I drank, I felt pleasantly surprised. It reminded me of the taste of summer strawberries freshly picked from the ground. Lifting my head with blood dripping from my teeth, I saw Sarah with two machine guns firing at a bunch of goons. Fuck me; she was like a madwoman but in control.

"Gloria, Val get out of here, we've got your backs!"

Suddenly, I saw Val walking toward me with a gang of men.

"Don't ask, I'll tell you later Gloria. Cables are you coming or what?"

Val said, staring at him. Cables turned around to look at Val before looking at me and saying.

"I'm sorry Gloria."

He turned back to Val.

"I'm staying. I have a few bones to pick with my father."

Sarah was yelling.

"Cables there coming! We can't let them have Gloria or Val! We can't have thousands of vamps walking in the daylight!"

"We'll catch up with them later'"

Gloria's pov

Val and the men lead me deep within the tunnels; torches were lit to show the way. The ground turned to a reddish-brown color where the blood of Val's kills had mixed with the mud. Walking on, I couldn't help but worry about Cables and Sarah. I felt guilty for leaving them.

"Val, where are we going to?"

"Home, deep beneath the canyon."

"The men will keep guard while we rest, my love; also, I have a surprise for you."

Sarah's pov

"Sarah, what the fuck's going on?" said Cables.

I looked at him

"I'll tell you once we escape, come on "use these."

She passed her men some hand grenades.

"Bury that part of the tunnel, and make sure the entrance is blocked."

"Yes ma'am."

We watched as the explosion caused part of the tunnel to collapse, and rocks and dirt blocked the exit.

"Come on, let's get moving! That should slow them down a bit."

Cables' pov

I felt devastated. Gloria had chosen him over me. I could feel my self-pity welling up and that wasn't manly. Shit, get a grip I thought I should have blown his fucking head off, but seeing her with him made me realize she would never forgive me. I would just have to wait and see what the outcome was. I looked at Sarah, wow she blew my mind. I thought she was the quiet type when all along she was this mean bitch. No wonder she loved being around Gloria, two of a kind and all. It was then I caught myself staring at her ass.

"Cables, come on, stop dragging yourself. I know you're hurting but we have to get to safety."

Hurting, I was suddenly fucking Horney. Must be the vamp genes. I smirked as I walked away with a mixed bag of emotions. One minute I was crying over Gloria, the next all I wanted was to fuck Sarah.

On the other side of the tunnel, Cables' father was pissed off. He looked at the tunnel full of so much rock and then at the sky.

"Scarp, find me another way into the tunnel. We've already lost a few men to them. Bastards! It will be daylight soon."

"Oh, fuck it Scarp, get back here."

He shouted.

"I will find another way. That dimwit of a son will be back soon. I'm sure of it, Scarp comes on."

Leaving the canyon in his 4x4 with a few fewer men, he went back to the city.

Chapter 10

Gloria's shock

Walking through the grand doors into a beautiful sitting room took my breath away. There was a fire burning in an antique grate where two comfortable red fireside chairs sat. Looking around the room, I could see large bookshelves full of books. On the floor lay a sheepskin rug and on the opposite side was a 4 poster bed carved out of the best wood. I froze and looked at Val.

"That's my bed, and that's my red dress. You saved it all."

"Yes, I had it put all in storage when you passed away; I thought it would make you feel more at home here"

Looking closely at the bed, I noticed a small body with brown hair. Looking closer, I pulled back the sheet.

"Hector, you bought our son back! I said sobbing"

"But how he was dead?"

Val looked at me.

"I'm sorry my darling, it's not hector, but he is an orphan. His name is Owen. I was going to bring our son back, but I changed my mind at the last minute, I didn't want him asking why he couldn't grow up with his mother. I didn't want to have to explain why you weren't there for two hundred years."

"How about you start from the beginning and tell me all about it?"

Sitting down on the chair by the fire, Val told me the whole long story.

Val's pov

The Book of Resurrected

After losing you, my heart felt dead. So I trailed the cobbled streets where our son had died. In case I could find his murderer. Walking into the tavern, I noticed a gentleman who was abusing a maid. Sitting down at the bar, I ordered a bottle of rum. A fine-looking gentleman who had been abusing the staff sat next to me. He pulled out the evening gazette.

"May I have a read, sir?" I said.

He grumbled at me.

"No! I'm reading it can't you see?"

Showing him the sharpness of my teeth, he quickly offered me the paper. I skipped to the part about missing bodies. The article read:

"Dead body found in the locks. Upon closer inspection, we found that her body had been butchered and that someone had used parts from different bodies and had sewn them together with surgical thread. He must have been a machinist for his precision cutting, how he chopped up his bodies was perfect. The woman was never alive. What had taken place was a grotesque abomination in the eyes of God. Inspector John Herbert was in charge of the case."

Leaving the tavern left me quite peckish, and I just happened to come across the fine gentleman from the tavern walking down a dark alley, pulling his coat up. Swooping down, I had my fill, so to speak.

Taking to the streets, I followed up on the areas that had the most deaths and it was in Whitechapel London, the same place where Jack had been playing. Jack was never a good man. He always whined about his murders being smelly, but he was tasty, I remember.

I considered my options and knew that I needed to see what was left. Smelling the air, I followed it to a university that used dead bodies in the name of science. Walking in was never my plan, so I took to being a mist that traveled down the corridor, till I came upon a small room with the remains of the body lying on a slab. On closer inspection of the body, I licked the threat. It tasted of old cotton, the sort you could find at a market.

That same night I met a couple of odd savory characters at the graveyard. I watched them dig a young girl's grave up. Bloody body snatchers. Licking my lips I thought I would have dinner. Yet there were quite chatty, they told me they were working for a fine man, which paid them well. His name was Frankenstein.

They said he was a scientific man of modern-day medicines and that he used the bodies for his experiments, and that he was a collector of old books, with that I feed on them gathering the scent of Frankenstein from their rough clothing. Pushing their corpses back into the grave they had just dug up made me chuckle. Well, it's only fair to end up the way they earned their dirty money.

After I got the sniff, so to say, I let my instincts take over. Standing outside an old abandoned hospital, I made my move. I looked around at old wooden beds, empty cabinets, and chairs that still rocked even though no one was there. Old books were open and pages were torn out and scattered on the floor. What a waste, I thought. Living forever gives you some degree of respect for belongings. Turning into a mist, I traveled along the long corridors till the smell led me to the morgue. Looking in, I saw a man in his late thirties experimenting on a dead body. If memory served me right, he was trying to use electricity to bring back the body. That will never work, I thought.

"Who goes there?"

"Pleased to make your acquaintance my name is Val, but others call me Count Dracula."

"Please don't run. You're Frankenstein right?"

"That's what some call me, and you are the master of many names. You are a legend in so many countries, yet I have the privilege of meeting you"

I showed him my teeth with delight.

"I'm looking for some help, maybe some knowledge of the whereabouts of an ancient book called *The Resurrected*. I'm thinking you have seen it, or know of it."

"Hum, let me think, there's a story I've heard of an old gypsy called Haglaid. He's very into dark magic and the occults. Here, come with me."

He led me to a library where he pulled out an old map.

"There, that's it. He lives on an island, south of here. Though be careful, there's a story that says those that walk on the island end up as ghosts and walk the planes forever. Legends have it that a school full of children were burnt to death in their school, their remains were buried on the grounds, and every night they walk the mountains in search of their murderers."

With that, I burst out laughing.

"I'm Dracula. Old folk stories do not matter to me."

"Oh yeah, I forgot for a second who you were."

"Maybe next time you shouldn't dump your bodies in the locks. Scotland Yard is on to you."

"Why thank you I will rectify that mistake."

With that, I left.

Heading for the docks brought back the same old memories as it was like yesterday. Sitting on top of a building, I watched the old sailors rushing about, dragging in their nets and preparing their boats for the morning trips. With that, I noticed him, a nasty-looking man, unshaved 5 foot 11, about 250lbs in weight, a proper rogue of the seas. Snarling, I picked up his scent. The smell of a child's blood, my child's blood, lingered on his ripped trousers. I turned into a dark mist and floated down onto the cobbled streets below. He was soon to be dead and I may just rip him apart piece by piece and send his remains to Frankenstein. My mind lavished the thought of tasting his fresh blood as I sunk my teeth into his neck, how my Gloria would act if she knew what I was about to do and how I was going to do it.

I made sure he saw me drop a bagful of money in front of him. I picked it back up and walked towards the alley by the tavern. The man couldn't help but follow. Lifting him in the air, I let him feel the full wrath of my anger. He let out a silent scream as my teeth sunken in. tearing him apart wasn't the hard bit, it was disposing of his time-consuming parts.

Dropping his remains into the ocean, I walked onto a passage boat paying the captain a grand amount of money to take me to the island, but not to wake me during the daylight hours.

Sitting down to think about the coming nights I had a lot to consider, yes I was hungry, but after two hundred years you learn to adapt and eat when required, and this was not the time. A gentleman sat next to me reading the newspaper.

"Hello there sir, it's a chilly night. Would you like a cigar?"

Thinking it was a kind gesture, I took it. The gentleman was dressed in a black suit with a top hat to match. He carried a fine brown leather briefcase, the usual attire for this period in time. Smoking the Cuban cigar, I said:

"May I help you?"

The man was straight to the point, polite but blunt, which I liked. He introduced himself.

"I'm Norman Fleetwood. I'm pleased to meet you Dracula. I work for an underground society called the Brotherhood of Truth. We have been around for thousands of years. We protect and serve the rights of the extraordinary gentleman of this world. We deal with people like Captain Nemo, Doctor Jeckle, and Mr. Hyde. As a lawyer in the field of insurance, we deal with the aftermath. We clean up, so to speak. We have lawyers serve our clients with diligence and respect. All information is kept deep underground in a very superior, reinforced vault. We will also protect you as you sleep. Let's get started, shall we?"

As he pulled out paperwork from his briefcase, I said:

"How much do your services cost?"

"For you sir, nothing in cash, but we may call on you from you from time to time to deal with rowdy individuals that cause our brotherhood harm."

"Considering the experience these gentlemen had in insurance, I agreed."

"Please sign here sir, and I'll let you enjoy the rest of the evening. With that, I went to my quarters, knowing someone was protecting me whilst I slept."

Chapter 11

The Island

The first thing I noted was the smell of the sea air, it was consuming. The blended potent smell of fish and fresh seaweed left me with memories of days out on the beach with my son and wife, those days before I became this creature, this creature of the night. Sitting on a rock cliff watching the ocean crashing onto the rocks below, I got to thinking of Gloria, in particular, and how her beautiful smile made me feel. I needed to stop feeling sorry for myself. As I had all the time in the world, I went exploring. Standing up, I brushed myself down and headed for the uninhabited part of the island. The fog had gotten thicker, but that didn't bother me. Nothing did. All I knew was that I wanted that book.

Gloria had given Hector the ring as a small token of her love. He was wearing it when we buried him. Looking through the woodland, I could see a small wagon. I could see that there were bottles, bottles of potions, they were hanging from branches. I noted the smell of death; it was so pungent, and I couldn't help but lick my lips in delight. Turning myself into a darkened mist, I slithered to the area where the wagon was.

Standing there, right in front of me, it was the man from the tavern, only the very man who had changed me into this vile beast, this beast that lived and fed on blood and flesh, who inhabited the night and its blanket of darkness.

"Who did you expect, a bloody Gypsy Val? I will always be your master. It was me. I gave you the gift, and this is what I get.

"You disguised yourself as an old tinker man and you gave me a disease, this wretched disease."

"A disease, yes, but it gave you immortality Val. It's not my fault you were beaten, you were the one that was weak my dear boy."

"Stop calling me boy!" I growled, "And I'm not yours".

Lucifer sat on a log and merely laughed.

"Your body was that of a weak man. I strengthened it. What I gave you was a gift; I gave you the blood of my brother so that he could live forever."

He laughed.

"So you see you are very much part of me."

I fell to my knees. I pleaded for him to take the gift back. Lucifer just turned away and walked into the tavern.

"I already know why you are here boy."

He chucked an old leather tattered book at me.

"And I want it back. You'll also need your son's ring if you want to bring your son back. Don't leave it too long; it needs to be done when the moon is high in the sky and when the bells chime at twelve."

Lucifer mumbled to himself, "Ungrateful sod." Then he was gone.

Turning the pages of the tattered book, I came upon the one I searched for.

"How to bring someone back from the dead?"

Yes, I could bite him, but I didn't want our son to be a vampire-like me.

Making my way back to the ship, I sat down on the deck chair outside my cabin.

"Are you okay sir"

I looked up to see Mr. Fleetwood, I gasped.

"Why isn't anything easy for me?"

"Sir, if I can be of any assistance, you only have to ask."

He passed me a cigar, which I lit and smoked in silence before going to my cabin.

Reaching back home, immediately I made my way to the graveyard. I knelt at the graveside and softly uttered,

"Hector for the last few months, I've done everything in my power to bring you back, but now I'm having doubts, I don't want you coming back and never growing up, your mother would never forgive me, I'm sorry my Son."

"So you couldn't do it?"

Lucifer said mockingly. I turned to him and gave him back his book.

"I'm pleasantly surprised; I never thought my brother was one for remorse."

I turned on him to take a swing at him, but he disappeared.

180 years later

Present Time

I looked at Val,

"So what about Owen?"

"I rescued him from a couple of vamps. They were about to rip him to shreds, so I took him and I've bought him up for the last two years as my own. I was hoping you would help."

I walked over and sat on the bed. I ran my hand through his soft, mousey brown hair. I couldn't help but think, what the fuck was happening? First, I have a husband and know a son.

Chapter 12

Cables' pov

Watching Sarah made me realize I needed to know what I was missing. What's the story with Dracula? I sat down in the tunnel for five minutes whilst Sarah checked up on her friends on her watch. I couldn't help but ask,

"So Sarah, what the fuck is going on with you and Dracula, and who the fucks are your mates? They weren't any civilians."

Sarah looked at me

"I guess it's about time I told you, seems as if we're at that point."

She put her ammo away in her backpack and sat next to me.

"My name is Sarah Fleetwood, I'm part of an underground brotherhood, which protects and looks after the rights of extraordinary gentlemen like Dracula. My predecessors met Dracula 180 years ago on a passenger ship. They offered him an insurance policy, which he signed. I am the great-granddaughter of Norman Fleetwood. We also work for the less advantaged and the elite. I need to tell you we have been watching your father for a considerable amount of time. I'm sorry to say this, but by the time he gets back, the facility and his building will have gone up in flames; several explosives have been set and should go off about now."

She looked at her watch. I froze; I didn't know what to say.

"For years, I was his only boy. I loved him, yet when he started experimenting on the public I just went nuts at him. I told him it was insane and sick, and he said it was all for the better, for the good. We rowed, and I was dragged away. My father and the other vamps in his coven, so to speak, thought it was a good idea to cross me with a bear as a form of punishment. I became one of his many experiments. I managed to break free. Returning was not of my doing."

Shit, I thought I had to go find out for sure. I jumped up and asked Sarah what the way out was. Enough was enough; I needed to see to believe it all.

Reaching the facility I got out of my car. Fuck, it was still standing, yes the outer shell was burnt out and there were a few burnt-out vehicles, but the mainframe structure was still standing. Sarah appeared by me.

"Fuck!" she yelled.

"We'll have to go in."

"Well, your father's gone nuts. He's rounding up all his vamps from the town and there's a big meeting taking place. Lots of limos are turning up with vamps spilling out of them. Yes, it was evident that something big was going to happen. Luckily we have a man on the inside."

"Where the fuck did you come from? I thought I left you in the tunnels."

"Yeah, right, I was going to let you go alone. I don't think so. It's my mission to keep everyone safe, so I hid in the back seat under your coat."

"Why shouldn't I protect you? We all have to earn a living, even the renegades like me."

Fuck, shit, I thought. This gal was amazing. Oh no, there go the vamp genes again.

"Come on, let's get in there," said Sarah, smiling.

"I need to get some of my work, anyway"

We went around the back end of the building and sneaked in through a side door, hoping not to be seen. I needed to find out what the hell was taking place, and I needed to do it without my father knowing.

Each damn time I enter this place I get Goosebumps, it's all that weird shit taking place. We walked on through the ground floor, where only a few vamps were taking notes.

"I'm hungry."

I said to Sarah, smiling. Morphing Into a werebear I ran off to feed. I was quite partial to vamp flesh, even though I was part vamp myself. Eh, it's only half cannibalism. I returned to Sarah with my mouth dripping with blood. She passed me a rag to clean myself.

"What? You don't like a bit of blood?" I said laughing.

"Come on, let's go!"

Sarah walked in front with a Heckler & Koch MP5SD strapped to her side. Integral silencer so she could drum any 9mm she wanted/found. Fucking cool, I thought, she has exquisite taste in firearms. Two minutes later, we were making a move through the corridors of the bunker. Suddenly, two men dressed in black walked out from a side room. I watched as she lifted the gun, took aim, and blew a whole straight through their heads. Moving on, we came to the first floor.

"It's going to get hard from now on. I need to go to my lab to get some tools".

Nodding my head in agreement, I headed upstairs myself.

Cables' father was named Mr. Nathan Courbet; he owned one of the biggest corporations in the city. When the infrastructure collapsed, Nathan sent out a treaty to all the other large companies in the city. Each would make a plea to work together for a better course. When the meeting took place, all seven were seated. Until one vamp, called the master walked in. He introduced himself, declaring his name to be Lucifer. If they were ever to survive the new world, the new order, then they would need him.

I hid inside a small broom cupboard which enabled me to watch and see who was entering the large conference room; I heard a small whimper come from behind. Turning, I saw the small girl from the container. She put her finger up to her lip.

"Quiet," She said.

"Come with me." I followed the girl; she led me through the back of the cupboard into a hidden room.

People or experiments should I say, we were huddled together by a fire that burnt in an old oil drum. What the fuck! I thought everyone had died in the fire, but obviously, he had not.

An older woman in the group declared that she had protected the others from the flames...

"We mutants, as I call us, have special talents. I can project a force field. Elaina over there can walk through flames unscathed. Mathew is part leopard, as it suggests, he can run fast. Nancy the little girl, she's a chameleon. We are all unique in our way, just like you when Nancy saw that lady of yours and when she looked in the container, she gave her hope. Nancy has expert hearing as well. She wanted to help. That's why she attacked the vamps to help you both".

Taking a seat, I listened to each of their stories and how their lives had been changed dramatically. I told them about Gloria and Dracula and also the tale of the Brotherhood.

I needed to find Sarah; I needed to know what the plan was.

"Look, we need to get out of this place. There's a side door on the bottom floor.

"I will get Sarah and we can meet up in the forest"

Walking back, I saw Sarah hiding behind a door with a couple of hand grenades in her hand. No, I waved like a Looney as she was about to blow up the conference room. I went to grab her, but it was too late. She launched the hand grenades. The red alert would start to go. What the fuck was I to do now?

Within all the chaos, and vamps screaming, I saw Sarah walking through the flames with her sub-machine gun, emptying its magazine into all who stood in her path; one by one they were blown away, like poetry in motion.

"Well, I'm pleased to see you."

She said with a cocky grin.

"Now let's get the fuck out of here."

Chaos was coming for us. Hearing my father yelling,

"Get the bitch. She cannot send all my works to go up in flames".

Seven top vamps walked behind him, all wearing black cloaks. The explosion had only killed their regular vamps and the assholes that helped them.

Running through the forest was not my plan, but damn, I felt free. We stopped to catch our breaths, and I don't know what happened next because I kissed her and she kissed me back. Oh fuck, I thought, I'm in for one hell of an experience. I think it was all the chaos that we had gone through, all the adrenaline flowing. We were both high on it. I pulled her close to me and felt her body contours as I ran my hands over her. Her very ample breasts felt great against my chest. As we kissed deeply, I heard her gasp with pleasure, that joyous moan that comes from the back of the throat. It felt so good to explore her mouth with my tongue. I found the buckle of her belt and loosened it, lowered the zip fastener and her trousers fell to her ankles. She repaid the gesture likewise for me. We both wanted this so much. The feel of her bush gave me such a boost. As I moved her panties to the side my fingers could feel how wet her pussy was, I couldn't wait to shag Sarah and entered her with my cock. Once my dick was deep inside her I discovered just how wet she was, and just how much she wanted me. The strokes were slow and meaningful at first. Oh, it felt so good the way she mouthed my neck. I didn't think Sarah was a vamp but damn I was half expecting teeth to plunge into my neck any second. While we were both having a grand time I figured I would do a little recon, so I moved one hand up her shirt, undid her bra, and began to massage a breast. Oh, her nipple was so hard and unusually large, I loved it and thought to myself I can't wait to suck on her nipples, but not now. My other hand went around back for her bum. So smooth and muscular, it was great how I could clamp my hand around her cheek and squeeze hard. Between that and when I started teasing her anus with my finger, she got more aggressive on my neck, pulled me closer, and tried digging her fingernails into my back. Her bum was so tight around my finger and felt awesome. After I slipped my finger up her bum I could feel it against my dick as she rode me. Then the urgency of the moment took over. I felt her body arching as we both reached that crucial moment together, that moment when the world seems to disappear and you only care for that moment. It was such an immense relief to squirt my sperm into her pussy. As of now Gloria and Sarah were 1 for 1 as to which was better sex. I can't wait to see how things evolve. Hmmm, can a werebear knock a girl up? Thinking about it could I have put a bun in Gloria's oven given she's a vamp?

To regain the occasion and catch our breath, we leaned against a tree. It was while we were leaning against the tree I heard a voice say,

"Well, look what we have here".

It was a woman's voice that I knew well. Both I and Sarah turned to see a blast from the past. Gloria and Dracula standing next to each other, Dracula had that cocky grin about him. Sarah and I didn't have to say a word. We both knew Val enjoyed watching the two of us going at it hot and heavy and we're positive he's hoping our performance will get Gloria all Horney and wet for when he gets a moment to shag her later in the day. However, Gloria looked like she was going to tear Val apart piece by piece. I went to say sorry, but she just burst out laughing.

"You two? It's okay I can work with this."

Dracula put his arm around Gloria and gave the side of her breast a gentle squeeze.

"Come on, there's a group of mutants waiting for us"

As we walked away, I couldn't help but think Gloria was lying.

"We got worried, so we thought we would follow your smell and god do you stink Cables, it's the bear part of you, take a goddamn bath," said Gloria giggling.

Sarah burst out laughing, and it made me wonder if she was aroused by my strong scent. Women, hey they can be mean bitches. Dracula merely walked silently ahead, smiling.

Gloria's pov

As we continued, we reached an old shack in the woods where we saw a group of people hanging about.

"Gloria"

Shouted the small girl, and she ran up and hugged me.

We were all getting to know each other when gunshots were heard. I zoomed in with my extrasensory sight,

"They're coming; everyone gets the fuck out of here"

Dracula looked at me and smiled.

"Shall we, my dear?"

With that, we changed; our fangs came out, and our eyes changed to a redder shade than normal. Cables morphed into a giant bear and Sarah stood her ground with her sub-gun at the ready.

"Everyone get into place"

With that, they came at us. There must be around 20 men firing machine guns, and some with dart guns. Two mutants went down. Sarah was dropping men like there was no tomorrow. I felt like I was in heaven. As I landed on one of them, we both fell to the floor. He was struggling to get his gun, but it was too late. I tore pieces of his neck out with my teeth and it tasted so divine. Watching Val blew me away, everything was in slow motion. My husband was ripping heads off and biting chunks out of them. I couldn't help but feel Horney. I mean, what can I say? He was hot as hell, and he was covered in blood. I took everything in, as it was slow motion. Cables were fucking up another vamp, ripping the vamp's arms off. Sarah was dropping men like a lawn mower. I could feel how wet my pussy was getting.

Running as fast as lightning through the trees with the wind in my face, I turned to see Val beside me. We stopped miles from the fight. Looking at each other with blood dripping from our mouths was so sexy, kissing him gave me Goosebumps, things heated up, and then it got rough, just how I like it. He pushed me against the tree and his hands traveled inside my trousers. He pulled them down, leaving my bare flesh exposed. God did me so want this. He inserted his hard cock into my pussy and he pounded me against a tree. Harder and harder, I screamed. Feeling him so deep inside me was fantastic. I bit him, tasting his blood as it trickled down my throat. With that, we both climaxed, I felt him explode inside me. I smiled. We both kissed some more and then he whispered,

"We best get back to see what's left."

He said, giggling.

Being a full vampire has its perks, like slowing down time, to us it could feel like a few hours, but in real-time it's not. Can all of us do this? Yes, but it takes practice and I could. Cables' father's men can do it as well. Reaching the shack, we caught Sarah and Cables celebrating rather nicely. Things had been heating up between the pair. I could tell by the way she watched him. I knew he felt guilty, but there was no need. I was a big girl who was in love with my husband. I wonder if seeing me with Val made Cables want Sarah more. I know seeing Cables with Sarah made me want Val more.

Making our way back to the tunnels, I couldn't help but think about how Cable's father got the ingredient. Back in Val's hiding place, Owen had just woken up.

"Owen, I'd like to introduce you to my lovely wife Gloria."

The thought of vamps hurting children did not make me so angry; I could never harm a child nor could Val.

"Hello, I said as he reached out and cuddled me before lying back in bed and falling back to sleep. Sarah sat in the armchair by the fire, as did Cables.

"Eventually, I have to go back and find out what the fuck is happening. I mean, what is the missing ingredient?" I said.

"Tell me what you are talking about."

Val replied, looking at me quizzing.

Sitting there, we told him everything that had taken place in the facility and how I was turned. Val looked at me seriously.

"Maybe I can clear up some of this mess," said Val.

Sitting on the edge of my bed, we went deep into a conversation.

"I believe the missing ingredient is my blood"

We stared at him.

"But how?" I said. He told us the story, taking us back.

"It was 180 years ago. Things were difficult then. I wanted to find a cure for the creature I had become, even if it meant losing you forever. Taking a few samples of my blood, I took them to a friend of mine, Frankenstein. Taking my blood and placing them on slides, we watched as everything we added bubbled, it was like the insides of a fire. It was hopeless. Frankenstein worked night after night till it became pointless. Putting the small bottles in my pockets, I left. But the night wasn't over yet. A crowd of people had gotten together to protest Frankenstein's experiments. They were carrying flaming torches. I tried to slip past, but I felt myself becoming hungry, so I waited in the darkness for an hour till the crowd died down. Watching them leave one by one, I saw a young lady fiddling with her purse. Walking up to her I offered to walk her home, being dark and all. We walked past the park and I pretended I needed to sit down, with that she sat next to me, it was then I bit her and she let out a scream, small but enough for a small group of men returning from the local tavern to hear her, with that they chased me. I heard one particular man swear a vengeance. The young lady was named Susanna Van Helsing, and she was somehow related to Gabriel Van Helsing, who was another one of my so-called brothers, who now vowed to kill me. It was then I figured that I needed to be more careful. So I moved here and set up home and placed my blood with the brotherhood and told them to watch it. I found out it had gone missing along with our pictures of us. Gloria and Cables looked at me and spoke.

"I know where the picture is. My father bought it on the black market, along with a few other things a few years back. It wouldn't surprise me if he was the one who had your blood."

"I bet my so-called brother Lucifer showed them how to use it."

"Bastard" Gloria replied.

"It would make sense. What could be more exhilarating than watching the world go into crisis as everyone turns into vampires"

"So, you didn't find a cure."

"No, my love, there isn't one, only one way to end, and that is death."

Chapter 13

Gloria pov

Being a vampire is cool, but it didn't mean I wanted other vamps to walk in the light of day. There had to be some form of order.

"We have to take them out, kill them all," I said.

That was going to take a lot of planning.

Thinking about supplies, I thought it was a good idea to go back to the gun shop. I told my husband I needed to be alone to make sense of everything. He sighed heavily before kissing me. Cables drove Sarah and me back. I told her I needed some me time, so to speak. They left together. I sat down on my basement floor feeling so stressed out, it was then I lost it. Throwing the table and experimental equipment in the air, I sat down to cry. So many memories were floating around in my head, my love for Val, my relationship with Cables, and the thought of being a vampire for eternity as well. I needed to be me again, and for that, I needed to ride.

Climbing on my bike, I smelt something unusual. It was coming from the sewage pipes. It smelt like trouble and I wasn't in a good mood. Checking I had my swords, I rode to the market. The smell led me to the sewage plant. Walking through the wet sludge, I came to an open area where different pipes came in from different directions. Taking a look around, I could see the leftover remains of people. They were piled in a heap on the floor. Hearing a noise, I hid in the shadows.

"It's feeding time boys."

I heard a man say, as he was dragging another man by his hair. Entering the open area he pushed the guy onto the ground. Watching closely, I saw 4 scarps climb out of the sewage pipes, each bigger than the last. Fuck, I thought, looking at the man whom I recognized from the market. He was huddled against a wall, pissing himself. He was an innocent human. Fuck this, I pulled out my swords and walked out into the open area, fucking scarps. I smiled because this time I was far meaner and far more than a normal vamp and I wasn't in a good mood.

Raising my swords, I chopped the tail off the first one. It screamed, coming at me with his sharp teeth dripping with flesh. I used my sword and chopped its head off, leaving nothing but a pile of a steaming mess on the ground. The other scarp ran at me and I grabbed his head and twisted it off. With the sword, I flew toward the 3rd scarp, bingo it went straight through its head. The last one hissed at me and then screamed in a high-pitched tone before running back through the tunnels. Picking up my sword, I turned to the man,

"I saw you buying human flesh from the market. Who the fuck was it for?"

Why would a human want human flesh?

"Okay, it's for my girl, she needs it. She lives on flesh like you but she's sick. She has some sort of disease which is killing her vamp genes, it's like she has a fever and her skin is falling off. I still need to give her blood, so I mix it up before feeding her"

Fuck me, I thought. I needed to see this.

"Okay, you can come out."

I knew my Val would watch me. He walked out with a cocky grin on his face. Walking over, he kissed me gently on the lips and turned to the man.

"Where is she?"

"At my house."

"So, you couldn't trust me?"

I said as we went to walk away

"It's not that. I couldn't leave you alone. I've been without you for nearly 200 fucking years Gloria. I'm not letting you go anywhere without me."

"I guess you saw me crying."

"Yes, I did, but I guessed you would work through it. I see you have." He said, looking at the pile of dead scarps on the ground. On closer inspection, Val looked concerned.

"This is what my blood has made?"

He said, kicking the remains.

"It's a fucking disgrace to me and you. How dare they? No one takes my blood and fucks with it without my permission"

Listening in a far tunnel was a terrified boy.

"Quiet"

I said.

"Someone's listening"

Within a second, Val returned, dragging a youngster by his ear.

"We could leave him, turn him, or could just kill him," I said.

"No, please, I heard nothing. I was running from cables' father's bodyguard. I'm one mutant from the container"

Looking at his brown eyes, Val sniffed.

"Shit, he fucking made you. How could he?"

"What?" I said.

"Gloria, look at him closely"

Looking at the boy, I noticed his brown eyes and mousey brown hair.

"What?" the boy said.

"Is he for real?"

"Yes, love. Weirdly it's our son, I have a suspicion he's a clone."

Well, if things didn't get any weirder.

"Let's get out of here, well take him with us."

I left my bike parked up whilst I got into Val's Porsche.

"Bit posh," I said.

"This is just one of many Gloria"

The boy and the guy got in the car too. It was a bit of a tight squeeze.

"Which way?"

"Down there on Norton Street. My house is on the left, number 3, through the gate. She's in the basement. Her name is Gail."

Walking into the house, we saw a double bed at one end with a small candle burning and a bowl of water beside it.

"Let me look," I said.

"Val, she changing. It's like she's morphing into something. She's burning up"

"Do you think she's going to die?" the man asked.

Val picked up the bag of flesh, opened it, took a lick, and spat on the floor.

"It's rotten. I can taste the poison. She's got septic. If we don't do a blood transfusion, she will die."

The young boy sat in a chair by the fire; he looked to be falling asleep.

"Val, we need to get some of my supplies from the shop so we can help her."

Val looked at the girl deeply.

"She's so young, maybe 15 or 16, who would turn a child?"

"I don't know, but we have to save her Val."

Leaving for the shop, Val looked worried.

"You know we could keep him. He is our son. He can help Owen." I said.

Val smiled, and then he put his arm around me.

"It will be okay, I promise."

On returning to help the young girl, the man had placed a blanket over the boy and he was using a damp cloth to cool the girl down. Pulling out the tubes and needle I connected one end to myself and then the other end to her arm.

"We need to drain and replace what she's lost."

Val looked closer

"I got this."

He sucked and spit till he couldn't do it any longer

"She's very weak but she's ready."

I pumped my blood into her. Watching as my blood trickled into her left me wondering about the boy asleep in the chair asleep.

'What if he's laying Val?"

"We'll find out tomorrow after we have both slept."

No, we don't sleep in coffins like the books say we use beds just like everyone else.

We watched the girl for a few extra hours before we decided she was okay. The man thanked us. Upon leaving, we made sure the guy had his meat checked. Why she never realized it was bad was a concern, though. Carrying the boy, Val put him in the car. Heading back, I was rather pissed off, but I was also dog-tired.

Later in the night, things seemed to go easier, but the clone son of ours got me thinking. He was quiet and more reserved, he watched us as we moved about. I was thinking he wasn't our son, but someone or something else.

"Tell me, is he kind to you?" I said.

The boy looked guilty

"Let me," Val said.

Val used his extra power to control the boy's mind

"Tell me; are you here to kill us?"

His reaction startled us.

"No, my father said I was to bring Gloria back to the facility, so they could experiment on her."

"Val Don't, he's just a boy. He's been brought up to hate and destroy. Val, please"

Val turned to the boy and looked at him before saying,

"We are your parents, you are loved and if anyone should dispute that they are lying, do you understand."

"Yes, father."

"Now go to bed, we're to have omelets tomorrow as a treat"

"Yummy" the boy replied.

"Dean, Can you look after Owen again"

"Sure boss"

Dean had been in Val's services for a long time. He was a butler and one of Val's best men.

"This has to stop Gloria, those monsters in the facility have no control over us, we are a higher form of a vampire and I will show them whom they are messing with, that vamp will pay for wanting to hurt you"

With that, we left.

"Gloria I have to tell you something"

I listened carefully

"We, being higher vampires, have the power to morph into something unique. Whatever happens, don't be scared. It is part of you; you need to let it out. Do you understand my love?"

"Yes, let all of my senses and bodily motions take over. Don't stop the transformation once it starts."

"Yes, we also need to find Cables and Sarah. They should be with the Brotherhood. I will show you the way. I'm going to teach you how to turn into a mist with thoughts only."

We started traveling at a fast speed, heading through the forest and stopping for a spot to eat. Then, carrying on, it was then I heard him in my head.

"How do you do that?"

"Magic, my love, it has a way. We're connected through our blood bond and our deep love for each other. Now, think of yourself as a cold breeze that spreads across a surface and as it touches a person's skin, now see yourself as a thunderstorm, darkness that floats down and engulfs the air."

I never realized how a mist could move so fast. We passed fields and streams traveling at a speed where the wind itself could not be seen or touched, only felt as it passed us by.

Deep underground below St Paul's Cathedral, a system of long tunnels lay. In the olden days, they would have been used to transport slaves to the tower. But now they were used only by the Brotherhood. Walking along we came upon a pair of massive iron doors with a symbol above them.

"The Brotherhood's cost of arms my love, two swords crossed with a dragon's head in the center. Come this way," said Val.

Taking in the details of the unground fortress gave me a chill that ran through my spine. The smell of oldness and antique furniture was spread out amongst the large rooms. Wooden bookcases were full of old leather bonded papers; each carried a special identification imprinted on them. Torches illuminated the place and made shadows that danced on the walls. Entering a grand room, I noticed a long antique wooden table. This was the centerpiece. Men dressed in monks' clothing sat around a blazing fire, discussing time and space. Cables and Sarah were sitting near the back of the room, deep in conversation. Cables lifted his head.

"All right, guys? You should see this place; it goes for miles and traverses the city."

Looking at him, I noticed Sarah was reading an ancient book. I leaned over to see the title, *Magic of the old world*."

"Is that stuff for real?"

"What do you think?" said an old monk.

"The Brotherhood has been around for a very long time, we have seen many rituals that included the casting of magic".

The old man wandered off into the labyrinth of many books. Sitting down next to Sarah, I told her what had happened and all the shit that was going through my mind.

"What the fuck, is he playing at cloning people, and how the damn did he do it?" Cables said.

"Cables calm down", Sarah said

"I think it's time I paid your father a little visit," Val said in a serious tone.

"Alone? I won't let you." I said, looking intently at Val.

Pulling me over to the side, he spoke in a serious voice.

"Gloria, for once stay here where it's safe. I know you can handle what may come, but I need to show them I am the boss of all vampires."

With that, I kissed him on the lips and said "Stay safe and if you take Cables don't get him killed"

Val sat down and told Cables the deal. He was on ball but I guessed he could have felt nervous being with Val alone.

We watched as Cables and Val left.

Cables' pov

I kept on waiting for Val to say something, so I said it first.

"I loved her; she was the only person who accepted me for who I was."

"I know, she's amazing. Her vibe is intoxicating, her attitude is one of a warrior and that of a beautiful goddess, she draws you in with her mysterious charm, and I will love her for eternity. I'm sorry I killed you, but you understand why?"

"Yes, I feel that way about Sarah now. What a woman, she does this thing with her tongue."

Val looked at me, and we burst out laughing.

I have to be serious with you. When I transform, and I will transform, you are not to get in the way. Do you understand me?"

"Yeah sure, keep out your fucking way, got it."

Driving to the facility, I couldn't help but wonder what Val was like when he was angry. Would he turn fully into something dark? I guess I'll find out.

Climbing out of Val's Porches, I pointed to the back entrance. I went to show him, but he was gone. All I saw was a mist traveling, I followed it. Val must have had his agenda because where I was going was not to my father; it was to the experimental rooms. I wanted to see how he cloned the boy.

Val's pov

Cables' father was working away in his office, nothing but boring paperwork. He stood up and made his way to his fridge which he kept in the room's corner, and grabbed himself a packet of blood lifting his head to see a man staring at him.

"Who are you?"

"I'm your worse fear sir, I'm Count Dracula. Some call me the devil, some call me the darkness. We need to talk about my wife."

"I was waiting for you. I didn't know whether you were still around."

"First, I'll give you a warning. If you don't listen I'll rip you apart."

"You know I could kill you and your bitch of a woman. She's been a pain in my ass for way too long."

That was the final straw. I picked him up and flung him across the room. He landed and shouted out

"Scarp, here now!"

I watched a slivering creature crawl into the room. It went to jump at me and I twisted its neck with just a thought. It fell to the ground, dead.

"You beast, he was my pet"

Cables' father's veins in his head palpitated as he came at me. That was when I transformed.

Cables' pov

I couldn't help but hear the discussion on my way to the lab. I thought about interfering but I remembered what Val said so I watched in silence, when I saw him transform I was blown away he had two massive grey wings and a scarily hard shell, his hands grew massive pointy claws and he was 60 foot tall, he filled the room, I was seeing a dragon.

"I will tell you, I am the oldest vampire ever and I will take no one's shit, especially when it comes to my wife."

I watched as my father cowardly sank to his knees.

Watching Val transforms back, he politely said,

"Do you understand the message?"

"Yeah, sure, I'll leave her alone. But I'll have you" he mumbled.

Val went to walk away when Cables' father yelled for his vamps. It was then I transformed.

Gloria's pov

I would not wait for confirmation, I was worried sick, and my husband had my back. Now it was time for me to have him.

"Sarah, I'm going. I can't stay and no nothing."

"Well, if you're going, so am I"

She grabbed her MP5 and a bag of mags.

"Sarah, I need you to listen and do as I say. We have to get there quickly, and that means I need to turn into a mist. I need you to cuddle me so I can bring you with me."

"I'm ready, let's go."

Sarah griped me tightly, I changed into a darkened grey mist, and together we traveled the landscape at 100 miles an hour

Landing by the facility, Sarah stood there.

"Did that just happen? It was fucking amazing!"

"Shush Sarah, I hear something."

Watching a group of vamps turn up in black 4x4 vehicles with the military as well pissed me off big time

"Something was taking place."

"Let's get a closer look at the fucking military"

With that, I and Sarah started to bust vamps' asses away. She was running and shooting. I was slicing vamps with my swords.

Walking through the doors was like a blood bath dead vamps and military men lay strewn across the ground. I smiled before I ran in, then I heard him.

"Couldn't help you, my love?"

I giggled.

"You should know dear, 200 years sweetheart"

Running through the facility, I didn't expect to see a dragon, wiping men out with fireballs and cables biting the heads off his father's men. I watched as a group of vamps tried to throw chains over my husband's grand body. He let out a great yell of pain as the chains were dipped in god's water.

"Don't you dare?"

Screaming my head off, the echoes traveled through the building as the changes took effect on me; I let all my senses work together.

"Remember relax let it happen, my love."

I heard him say through the pain.

Falling to the ground, I felt my backbones crack. Growing to 100 times the size of a normal dragon, I stretched out my black wings and opened my mouth, which was twice as large as my husband's dragon form. Transforming into a dragon was amazing. My husband looked at me with respect as I blew out a fireball. Sarah jumped on my back. She was a hell of a climber.

"Come on!"

She said, blasting vampires apart with her MP5.

"We need to burn the facility to the ground. It's the only way to stop the experiments," said Sarah, as she was shooting down vamps. Cables' father was running away when Val gripped him.

"Where do you think you are going? We need to talk away from this place."

I watched as Val dragged him up in the air with his claws and took him out of the facility.

Chapter 14

Val's conversation

Landing on a top of a cliff, I transformed back into my usual being. I couldn't help but wonder if he was real or just another fucking clone.

"I want to know how you cloned my son."

Pacing up and down was not my thing, but it seemed rather appropriate for this time of night.

"Okay, Okay, Okay, but you won't like it," he said.

"I Know!" I yelled.

"We dug up your son's remains. We used his bone stems to make a live, living, organism. From there we grew him in a test tube,"

Val then said "Is my son okay? He means everything to me."

"I wouldn't call him your son and I wouldn't have sent him to find my wife.

Look she has the key to walking in the day and I need it, with her blood I'd be the top dog in the industry. I will have full control over all the vampires; I will have an army, and the use of many factories to harvest humans."

"This is all about the money and fame for you. My family is not to be used for YOU'RE profit"

"I could make your head of my vampire army; it will come with everything you ever wanted."

I looked at him. I knew then he had to go, plus I had a sneaking suspicion he wasn't the real McCoy. I wasn't going to go through that again. Plus I was already head of the vamps, including him. He just didn't get it. Fame had gone to his head.

Studying him, I watched as his veins pulsated. It was then he tried to lift me in the air, and that was his ultimate moment.

"Do you think someone could use my power against me?"

I gripped his head and used my fingers to press his eyes in, blood-flowed out from his sockets, and with a pop, his head exploded.

"Fucking asshole!"

Back in the facility

Sarah had invited cables to jump on my back as I lit the place up; watching vamps scream as they burnt to death made me feel in control.

"Gloria, meet me at the brotherhood."

With that, I worried. Transforming back into my original form left me naked.

"Stop staring Cables!" said Sarah.

"Well, did you see the size of her, Sarah? Fucking hell, she was meaner than Val, and he was fucking huge. Talking of which, where is he?"

"He's waiting at the Brotherhood for us. Come on, let's get going."

We stood and watched as the flames spread through the building.

Cables' pov

I couldn't help but think about what Val did to my father in the end. Did he kill him or let him go? I drove in quiet; both girls were wrapped up in a blanket in the back seat, and both looked knackered. Reaching the underground entrance I couldn't help but admire the history of the place, pushing the large doors, we went over to where Val was standing, he was smoking a Cuban cigar; he looked at me and shucks his head.

"How?" I said.

"You better all sit down. What I'm going to tell you will shock you all."

Five minutes later

"A fucking clone, I don't believe it, how did you know?" said Cables.

"I guess I can smell them, they give off a toxic smell of chemicals, which must be what they used to bring him to life, plus he was too eager to please, and kept talking about the plans. I'm sorry I had to take him out Cables"

I couldn't help but be shocked. We were talking about a whole new thing and was there more than one facility in this shit world. The thought scared me, but I had to mention it.

"What if there is a facility in every city?"

"Wait, we have a map if I can find it, and we can use one of these spells from that book," Sarah said excitedly.

I was slumped in a chair watching the fire dance.

Fuck it, I'm going to find him. That father of yours is one dead vamp walking," I said.

Whilst Sarah fetched the book, I couldn't help but think about what was to come.

"Here, I have it."

Sarah came running back and placed a comprehensive book on the table. We sat down to observe the power of magic which the pages contained and the effect it had on the map. Then a man arrived, one brotherhood asked to speak to Val.

Val walked over to where the man was standing. He had blood stains all over him.

"Sir, we have a problem. Your home has been broken into. They came up from beneath through the underground tunnels.

Dean said it was Cables' father's vamps. He fought a few off, but they beat him. He died on the way here, sir."

We watched as Val's eyes got redder with anger and we knew what was to come

"Just tell me," Val said in a deep voice

"They took your boy's sir"

"Fuck it; I'm done with these fucking half bread creatures!"

I knew by his expression that he was talking about vampires.

"Gloria, come on, we need to get our boys back and fucking kill every fucking vamp that gets in our way. Sarah, find out where the other facilities are located. Cables stay guard in case they come for you both; they may find a way here."

We left with nothing but revenge on our minds.

Reaching the tunnels was not an auspicious occasion. Footprints and dead vamps have covered the ground. Sniffing the air for fresh blood, we followed the stench. It led us to a big hole in the ground.

Jumping down, we traveled a mile deep, pretty exhilarating for me stopping at the bottom. I couldn't help but kiss Val passionately; the thrill of killing vamps was vibrating through my bones. He smiled at me with a sweetness I couldn't resist, checking no one was about I famished his hot muscular body, Tearing his clothes off piece by piece, I pounced on him and straddled his hard manhood and wrapped my body around it, letting out a deep moan as I moved up and down. With that our vampire instincts took over, we bit each other and blood trickled down our bodies. Rubbing the blood into my bare chest, he kissed me passionately.

"Damn, that was a rush!" He replied.

I giggled.

"What can I say? I was feeling randy," I replied.

"I could tell," he said.

Walking on, we came to an opening. Taken by surprise, we saw small gangs of people having their blood harvested. Tubes were directly connected to large metal drinking vats. Looking closely at the people that were being used, I noticed a few had a few drug disorders.

"Bad blood."

I said to Val. thinking back to when we saved the young girl gave me clarity as to where the flesh had come from. I could have let them die, but at the moment we had other more important things.

"Come on, let's move on," Val said.

Staying closer to the walls, we transformed into a dark mist and drifted down the corridors of cages. We heard sounds and screams bellowing down the corridors. What had we walked into, some sort of massive operation? The voices grew louder the closer we got. They were shouting win, and 20 cigs for the vamp to win, no 30 for the scarp. What the fuck? They were betting on a fight. Feeling the blood in my veins start to bubble, I felt a tremendous urge to rip apart everyone in the area.

"Val, what the fuck's happening here"

"Cage fights love. They do it to trade in goods. I've seen it before in the olden days in the Gypsy camps. I thought it was an old-time tradition. It's still about."

"Gloria, let me look for our sons; you need to let off a bit of steam and calm your blood lust after you can join me"

Smiling, I agreed.

Picking up the smell of Oliver from one of the larger vamps, Val disappeared into the crowd.

The cheers for the vamp in the cage grew louder and more demanding. Hundreds of Vamps rattled the large arena cage.

"Who's next to beat George the Vamp? "Said a small vamp with a mustache and a long fur coat. He looked like a local pimp. Smiling, I thought, why not?

"I'll go in the cage."

I raised my hand.

"We have a challenger. Are you sure, little lady, wouldn't you be better in the streets, he winked at me? Wanker, I thought.

Taking my leather coat off, I handed it to a young vamp girl who was standing at the front.

"Don't worry; I'll be less than five minutes."

"Good luck," she said.

"Hi sweet checks"

Turning to see the vamp in the cage, I grinned like the Cheshire Cat. The bigger, the better I thought.

He was the size of a football player 6 foot plus I'd say; he was in his late 20s, fit as hell. He had muscles that popped from his ripped t-shirt. I smiled and with that; I ran at him. It was like poetry in fucking motion; I flipped him onto his back. He jumped up and punched me and I fell to the ground with a loud thud as my head hit the ground; it was then I felt myself become alive. My blood bubbled, and I let myself go wild. The voices and rattling grew louder. I licked my lips with delight. He landed on me, with his full weight, but that didn't matter. Leaning forward, I head-butted him and he fell backward. I bounced back up like a panther and did a flying kick to his head. He stumbled even more. That was my cue. Jumping up in the air, I lunged myself at him, wrapping my legs around his neck, and with my hands, I snapped his head off in one fine motion. His body tumbled and twitched as it hit the floor. Launching his head into the crowd made me giggle.

What is ecstasy! It's a feeling of bliss, I loved killing. What had I become? Who was I?

"I believe you are my wife."

I heard my husband say.

Leaving the cage, the girl passed me my coat, and she grinned. I raised my fist and said,

"Girl power and all"

"Fucking bitch, you don't think we're letting you out of here."

The small vamp replied. Vamps are like Muppets on a string, one gives orders the others follow. They came at me one by one, then I let out a scream and tumbled to the floor, I was transforming, and with it came a lot of dead Vampires. I left a small group of vamps that had hidden behind the seats speaking in a loud clear voice I said:

"My name is Gloria Dracula, wife to Count Dracula, you will listen to me or I'll rip every fucking one of you apart. Have you seen two young human boys being dragged this way?

The girl that was holding my coat pointed to the room down to the left.

"It's where they train them."

"Who trains them?"

"The big boss, I saw one of his goons come this way with two boys,"

Walking off, I nodded my head to the girl.

"Gloria, you need to come and see this. I'm in the room down the corridor to the left."

I opened the door to see cages upon cages with small, dirty street children. They had been gathered up like wild animals. I looked closely before turning to Val with a worried look on my face.

"Val, what's going on here?" Gripping the vamp by the neck, he ordered him to speak, "Tell her what you told me about the children."

The children are changelings; they are the boss's children. When they transform, they turn into scraps, the older they get, the bigger they get."

"Those are not children," I said.

"No, they portray that to catch their prey," he said, laughing.

"Well fuck me!" I was blown away.

"So you think that's funny do you?"

"Well yeah, it's fucking hilarious, because you think your son is a human clone."

Shit, we had to find Oliver and quick.

"Where is he?"

I said as I punched him in the face. Val had still had hold of him and was grinning like the Cheshire Cat.

"He's been taken to the underground facility, under the Crown Building; you won't kill me will you?"

"No"

I said, smiling. At that, Val snapped his neck and ripped his head off.

"What about them?" I said, looking at Val.

Val looked and gazed at the children.

"Fuck'em, we haven't got time."

"Val," I said.

"We can't leave them. What if they are children and he was lying?"

"Leave them well come back I promise."

Walking out, I didn't look back. I couldn't. We walked back down the tunnel and climbed out. Turning into a mist, we traveled to the Crown Building. "Wait," I said, something's not right. It was too damn quiet. I couldn't see or hear any local street yobs, let alone the mafia vamps that gathered on street corners.

"We have to go now," he said before they kill them."

What was Val seeing that I couldn't? Val told me.

"They're building an army of vamps but they need human boys to be sacrificed to Lucifer for him to give them power"

"Power for what?"

"To walk in the daylight."

"It's Lucifer. He lies like fuck to get what he wants. He loves making trouble for me. He's a total wanker!"

With that, we heard a laugh, turning to see a man in a white suit smoking a cigar and laughing as he turned into a mist.

I felt my blood bubble inside as my temper was becoming uncontrollable.

"What a dick!"

"Your right about that. I think we should go stake the place out and see what we are up against there."

Walking along, I couldn't help but think about the city and how it had changed in the last few years.

"Val, how many vamps do you think there are in this city who hear Cables' father's bullshit?"

Here, in this city, there are a few million vamps, maybe more, but add it together with the other cities. I'd say at least a billion."

"Do you think Cables' father will take full control of them all?

"No, not by a long shot the originals vamps won't have it."

Val's pov

I couldn't get it out of my head that the clone boy was a scarp. How could I have been so wrong? I must be losing my touch, I thought. Gloria was worried sick all the time, and I could tell that her anger was becoming uncontrollable.

Spotting a group of vamps, we followed them. They lead us to an underground entrance which opened up into a large chamber. Thousands of vamps were standing in a crowd, patiently waiting for the sacrifice to begin.

Lying on a slab was my boy Oliver, not the clone, which had me even more curious. Where was the clone, and who was he with? Someone was fucking with my head and I didn't like it.

"Gloria, I have an idea. I'm going to create a diversion, I need you to take Oliver and get out, have you got it"

"Yes, I got it. What then? We take full control?"

"No, not yet. We need to draw up a plan of action with Sarah and Cables.

Gloria's pov

I knew I could have controlled myself better, but I'm the type of girl that thinks fuck it.

"Val, I can't control the dragon in me. She coming out whether you like it or not.

I gathered that, when I read your mind, okay, fuck the diversion, it was only an idea, anyway."

Transforming or morphing, so to speak, felt intense, but the feeling was so amazing. I didn't even know I could fly. I Circled the Chamber and let out a fireball. The air was engulfed with flames and smoke. Looking down at my boy, who had been heavily sedated, I felt so many emotions for him. He was our son. Whist I was deep in that trail of thought, I saw something that took me by surprise, several vamps were standing in the darkness of the shadows wearing black cloaks, watching as we were destroyed everything, We had killed so many vamps it had become a bloodbath, many were screaming as they ran towards the entrance to escape.

"Val, who are they?"

I said, as our minds connected.

"They are the law."

"So why aren't they doing anything"

"I think they like to see what's going on, and then figure out if and when they should interfere."

"Why haven't they stopped us?"

"Because they knew we were coming here, it's an all setup. They have wanted to downsize the population of vamps for ages."

"Where's our boy come into it?"

He was the bait, Hun. They didn't want to do the dirty work themselves, so they fed some bullshit story to Cables' father knowing he would come for our son and we would go nuts."

"And Lucifer, where does he come into it?"

"I'm afraid he's one of the original vampires. He is the one I told you about."

"They only interfere when someone threatens them. It was one of them that gave me the necklace. She said it was an emblem for the sacrifices I made for true love."

"How did they become vampires?"

"They were born vampires"

With that, Val swooped down and picked up Oliver and turned himself and Oliver into a darkened mist, and swept Oliver away to safety.

I looked at the vampires who had been watching the whole showdown. One of them was a woman with long black hair. She smiled and nodded before they disappeared into the darkness.

Chapter 15

For thousands of years, Lucifer and his kind walked the earth preying on the vulnerable people of the cities but keeping the number low and manageable so they could go unseen. Lucifer had a sister called Mercy; she is one of the most beautiful vampires in existence, with her long black locks that bounced on her cold breasts. She coaxed many a man by her charm and good looks.

Mercy and her brothers all had one special ring that was made for them by an old Gypsy woman. They were told they could only use the ring to walk in the daylight hours once a month. Mercy became good friends with the G ypsy women and told her of the troubles she had faced in the last thousands of years. The Gypsy woman on her deathbed cast an ancient spell and told Mercy, out of love, that she could walk every day with her ring. Mercy wasn't a ring person, so she had hers made into a sunstone necklace, which she kept for decades on her neck.

Two hundred years ago, she had a daughter called Gloria, whom she kept a secret from her family. Lucifer and Mercy had a massive row over wealth. To stop Lucifer from finding out about Gloria, she took it upon herself to use a spell to wipe Gloria's memory and replace it with a fake one. When Gloria was 21, she married a man that was rich and charming. His name was Count Valentine Dracula. When mercy found out what Lucifer had done, she offered Dracula her sunstone as a form of apology for her brother's misdeeds.

Gloria pov

The women had left an imprint on my mind, like a memory, that had a long time been locked away in a treasure cave. Reaching the Brotherhood, I found Val had placed Oliver down on a sofa. Cables walked over to me and asked if I was okay. I was, but I was confused and concerned. Sitting on the sofa next to Oliver, I stroked his hair as he fell asleep. Val walked over and I looked at him with tears in my eyes.

"Val, I have a strong feeling there's something about that woman that keeps me looking back through my memories. It's like I have known her for a very long time but something is blocking the full memory."

"I know what happened," Sarah said, butting in.

"I read it earlier, it's an ancient blocking spell used thousands of years ago by ancient witches, and it was used as a form of protecting someone's thoughts." What the fuck, why would a person use that on me, and for what reason?" Cable was standing there whilst Val told him about the scarp children and the whole setup. We all took to a seat. We needed a plan, we needed to find the truth, and I had to find out who that woman was.

An old man approached us.

"Ladies and gents we have made you all a bed up in the back quarters please take some rest." Lying on my bed cuddled up to Val had me thinking I needed to go look in the archives for anything they had, any information on the originals. I slowly got up and proceeded to the library. Climbing a bookcase, I grabbed an old-looking book that was bound in brown leather. Feeling it, I had a creepy feeling. It was skin, it read. *Vampire History* dated back to the 13th century.

"What's that you go there in your hand?"

I turned to see Cables sitting at a table with loads of books as well. I think it is an ancient book about how it all started."

"Gloria, I want to apologize for my actions and the way I acted with Sarah, I should have told you about my feelings for her." I looked at him and smiled "it's okay; it's me who should say sorry for hurting you. That night I was raped left me scared but when Val showed me my past self, I realized he was the invisible force and why he did it to me, to him it wasn't rape, and it was his way of showing me he loved me, plus I loved it."

"I could tell," he laughed.

With that, I said goodnight and took the book with me.

Chapter 16

The following night I set to reading, whilst Val played with Oliver in the sitting area. They were talking about the upcoming new boarding school and the classes he had. Deep down, I think he knew we were creatures of the night, but it was better than his previous life.

Sarah and Cables were cuddled up on the sofa, playing, fighting. Brushing my hand across the book, I opened it

A long time ago, a group of vampires ruled the earth; each lived in different parts of the world, each following their own secret set of rules. Lucifer, the oldest brother, was a flesh-eating monster who had no remorse for the ones he chose to eat. When war broke out, he took it upon himself to kill the King of Greece and take his place. Thousands of men were turned into vampires and the elite army grew. Lucifer's sister Mercy couldn't let it carry on, so she went out on a quest to gain the power to override her brother. Traveling to the fairest planes, she met a man who told her an old folk story about a Norwegian dragon that lived in a deep cave that could help her. Entering the cave, she was met by a handsome man who used his charm and seduced her. He gave her two gifts. One was his power to transform into a mighty black dragon. The other was a wish that she keep close to her chest, in the hope it could be used at a better time.

Gloria pov

Sitting in quiet, I carried on reading, so much history of a time long gone. Sarah came and sat next to me

"I did the magic on the map last night to look for other facilities, but getting the ingredients was a little weird. I and cables had to go on a late-night trip."

"Where to," I said staring at here

"Do you know the place where all the homeless hang out? It's near Walnut Avenue. There's a small shop that sells potions and bit and bobs from times long ago."

"Is that still going?"

"Yeah, I think the woman in there uses magic when she senses large groups of vamps coming near the shop. Anyway, she would only allow me in, Cables had to wait outside"

"What does she look like then?"

I was sure it was an old man called Norman that had owned the place.

"I'd say she's about thirty with long black hair; I admit she was really beautiful. I'm sure she said her name was Marcy or Mercy, something like that. Anyway, I asked her about finding things and she gave me this crystal on a string. I went to pay her but she and the shop were gone. I was left standing in the street with Cables staring at me with his gob open." Sarah was staring at me because even I had my gob wide open. "Are you fucking serious about the entire building?"

"Damn right," replied Cables as he walked over to us.

"Anyway," Sarah said, punching Cables for interfering, we got back and opened the map, spreading it all over the table. With the crystal, we said a spell from the book and this is what happened." Sarah opened up the map and what I saw took my breath away, the map had lit up and Sarah had used a red pen to join up the lights. What we were seeing was the devil's pentagon; Val had joined us and was taking in all the details.

"Well fuck me!"

He said in a serious tone. I knew then that we had a lot of work ahead of us. Every different facility had a different boss. Oliver had come and jumped on my lap and for that brief moment, the thought of fighting and killing was out of my mind. A few hours later, Oliver had been whisked away by the Brotherhood for his protection of Val's orders.

Traveling back to the gun shop, I needed to collect as many weapons as I could. Val and Cables had been loading up with ammo while I was collecting my papers from the experiment, when it happened, I fell backward, and lucky Val had caught me. I was having a flashback of a woman and myself as a kid running on a beach together we were having a picnic surrounded by the sound of the waves.

"Gloria, are you okay?"

"Did you see Val, that woman that was there from the other night?" Val walked over and kissed me softly on the lips. He knew I felt distraught.

"I need to know who she is to me, Val."

"I know, my love, we do. We will find out together, but we have to find Cables' father and that scarp boy and destroy the changelings somehow."

Cables' father's pov

Pacing up and down, I was bitterly angry. I had planned to walk in the daylight that coming day, but that bitch of a girl and her fucking husband had ruined my plans.

Sending a group of vamps, I told them to collect the children. If they weren't kept safe, they would die. They were the last of their kind. I ordered them to meet me at the facility's headquarters, which happened to be in the old iron foundry, deep underground. I arrived at the headquarters and sat down on my comfortable leather chair, thinking about Gloria and how unique she was. She would make a noble experiment to do an autopsy.

Gloria's pov

The following night we all went out together, leaving well equipped. We knew we needed to find other vamps, but who would join us in the war against Cable's sicko father? I was hungry for flesh though, so we stopped by the market for a bite; I didn't like that stallkeeper that sold dodgy meat. It wasn't the best meat, but it was fresh. Walking through the market, we bumped into the girl we had saved a few nights back. She was hanging with another vamp. They were discussing my and Val's small visit to the underground cage fight.

"She was amazing."

I heard one of them say.

"I agree," said Val, butting in on the group's conversation.

"Well, how did she do it? We want to know. Can we all transform too?"

"Yes, you can, but it takes practice and a quiet mind. Learn to let go and let the changes take place"

"Can you teach us, we know of a place where we can learn?"

For a while, Val paced up and down considering his options and what was our best choice of action. We needed to get as many vamps on board as possible, so we told them the truth, that Cables' father was the only one who would benefit from walking in the daylight. That he would never share with them, how he could do it I made them think that Lucifer had the solution as I didn't want them knowing about my necklace, some secrets are best left out.

"I knew it. I was there when he was giving a speech. I knew he was full of shit. I was there when you were going nuts. You were so cool. "Said one of the male vamps. He was in his thirties, the usual type of black jacket, blue jeans, and brown hair with a small quiff at the front.

"I want to help," said the girl.

"You helped me when I was sick, so let's say I'm repaying the good deed, we'll join won't we Smog?"

"Damn right we will. I hate that stuck-up ass."

Looking at Val, I gave him a little smile. I was feeling a little weird.

"Val," I said "someone watching us."

"Let me."

I said "No, I want to"

"Be careful then"

Walking into the alley, I noticed a woman standing in the darkness. She had been watching me for some time.

"Hey who are you?"

"Just a friend," she said.

"So why can't you just speak, stop following me, or ill ripe your head off with my bare hands," I growled.

"Gloria, who the hell do you think you're talking to? I didn't wait hundreds of years for that talk." when she said that I stared at her, and was intensely looking at her neck why was she wearing the same necklace like mine.

"Who are you?"

"I'm someone that's watched you grow up, who's always been there in the shadows watching you. I couldn't show myself till now Gloria, it was for your protection, but you are more than able to handle him now."

"Whom?"

"Lucifer."

I went to ask her more, but she had gone. I sank to my knees just to be picked back up by Val, Cables, and Sarah ran over to where they found Val holding me tightly.

"Val," I whispered.

"Yes my love"

"I think she's somehow my mother from times gone by"

Mercy's pov

It broke my heart watching my daughter from the shadows never interact.

200 years ago

Things may have been simpler, but it wasn't for the children that lived in Hawkins Orphanage. Children were left to defend themselves, only given scraps of food and a small heap of porridge a day. Saving children was what I could give back. I would rescue them and place them in a better family, wiping both parents' and children's minds and giving them the best of a loving bond. Except for Gloria, I would watch her sitting on an old wooden swing, talking to her invisible friends. I would leave her food parcels which she hid in an old tree stump. She was such an exceptional child, sharing what I'd given her with her friends, which they all kept quiet or a beating would take place, until one day I noticed Gloria had stopped sitting on the swing. Changing into a mist, I traveled through the long corridors of the orphanage. The children that were left were sleeping quietly. I sniffed the air and caught Gloria's scent. It was a sweet smell of flowers. Following it led to the basement, and I grew more worried by the second. The basement was an inhospitable place; with walls that were covered in cobwebs. Looking closer, I saw a small door to the side. Opening it left me feeling disturbed; it was a small cloakroom where the old chimney sweeps left their brushes. There in the corner was Gloria, bruised and battered and cold. She was barely alive. I lifted her out and misted her back to the hotel which I had acquired at an earlier date; I admit the owner tasted lovely. Laying Gloria down softly I had a choice to make. I didn't want to change her, but I needed her to live through her ordeal, with a small slit to my wrist, I trickled a little of my blood into her little mouth and whispered "Gloria you are strong", praying that she would heal. I watched and waited. As an older vamp, I knew how much blood to give. Reading her mind, whilst she laid there, unveiled the events of that day.

Gloria's pov

I hated this place, it was always cold and I noticed that my friends were going missing. The only good thing that happened was the gift of food I was receiving. It was a cold autumn day; the leaves had left a fine, multi-colored blanket on the ground. Wearing my ripped duffle coat with the one button and black laced boots, I walked off to the old tree stump. Kneeling to gather the bread and fruit that was wrapped in a white sheet when a humongous hand gripped me. It was the owner of the orphanage. I let out a scream, and he covered my mouth. Dragging me away by my arms, I looked at his big fat face that had turned a shade of red. Screaming

"How dare you steal food from our kitchens?"

He hit me, and that was the last thing I remembered.

Mercy's pov

Watching Gloria heal as she drifted into a deep sleep I knew I was going to have to rip him apart piece by piece.

Leaving the hotel with the doorman watching Gloria I went back to the orphanage. Sniffing the air I picked up a male's odor, it gave off a potent smell, this guy I was not going to eat, he stunk horribly. The fat gentleman who was bold and looked like he needed a bath sat in an old wooden chair eating my food parcel. Demisting back into myself, I approached him, as his face turned in shock.

"Who are you? Get out of here," he said, as he was profoundly sweating.

"So you like my food," I said, showing my fangs.

He dropped the bread and went running to the entrance.

"There's no point in running. I don't have the time to waste on you, but I like to feed the pigs at the local farm."

With that, I gripped him, and we went for a ride. Do you know pigs will eat anything? They only leave the teeth and hair as they can't digest them. I didn't want him to scream, so I took it upon myself to eat a delicacy, tongue. As I pulled his teeth out and ripped him apart, I told him of his misdeeds and how he tasted.

Leaving the farm, I went to meet a dear friend, who had just lost his job as a schoolteacher, so I offered to fund the orphanage and give him a job as the new owner. The news was that the old owner had disappeared with the funds from the Christmas fate. Reaching the hotel, I went up to my room where Gloria had stirred. Not wanting her to remember such an ordeal, I gave her a whole new life. Why shouldn't every child be loved? Waking, Gloria wrapped her arms around me, giving me a loving hug.

" Mummy, I'm hungry," she said.

10 years later

Gloria had become a beautiful lady with a life full of special memories. She courted a fine gentleman by the name of Count Dracula.

Chapter 17

Present Day

Leaving as a small group, we traveled to an abandoned underground train station. There was an old train compartment that we used as a resting area. The following night, we set up an area to use as a training camp. Each area had a learning area, a space to transform, and a place to develop their skills; if we were to grow an army, we had to be ready to fight. While we trained, Smog had gone out to round up the wayward and strays from the cities out backs. Each vamp would learn how to handle themselves against another vampire. Each would become the best they could be and Val would have to use a little of his blood to connect, so we were all connected

Sarah's pov

As I sat in the underground train compartment, I couldn't help but read the book on magic. Reading the words on the pages made me feel different as if I was becoming a vessel for the pages to dwell in. Committing the passages to memory, one by one, sitting there reading I noticed myself floating. The words were leaving the book and traveling up my arms then disappearing. I called out for Cables' and he came running in.

"What the fuck?" He said.

With that, I stopped reading the pages and floated back down to the ground Cables gripping me by the shoulders I turned to face him.

"Sarah," he said. "Your eyes are like blue diamonds, but so bright"

"It's the book," I said. I think it's bringing itself to life in me."

"Do you think it's dangerous?"

"No" I heard Gloria say from behind me.

"May I?"

She took my hand and ran her hand against my arm.

"I have a feeling and I don't know how, but I think the book has found its new home."

"There's an old folk story about a powerful witch." Said Val,

"The story goes the witch contained the power to kill an original. The problem was, that Lucifer wanted her dead. So she transported herself into a book. By all counts, he's been looking for her ever since"

"What's her name," I said.

"Madelyn."

"Have you tried to speak to the book? It may well be her," Val said, looking at cables then Gloria. We all took a seat

"Madelyn, are you with me?" Sarah's eyes lit up.

"Yes Dracula, I'm here, I see you are well," she spoke in a soft voice.

"Madelyn, we need your help. Lucifer is controlling Cables' father, and with his help, they will build an army of vampires. If they find out the secret of how Gloria walks in the daylight, what is left of civilization will be no more," Everyone sat there quietly waiting for a reply.

"I have been reading Sarah's mind, she will need to transfer me to Gloria's mind. Sarah's mind is not strong enough for my knowledge and spells to stay more than a few hours. Gloria's body is young but her mind is old. Once I pass into Gloria I will need time to become one with her."

Gloria walked up to me, took my hand, and connected to my mind. I felt a power source leave my body and enter her, and with that, I passed out.

Madelyn's POV

The originals had been around for 1,000 years, mostly eating and staying in the darkness of the shadows. The year was 1692. The world was struggling with famine and people fought in the streets. It was the year of the Salam Witch Trials, which sent the entire world on a mass hunt. Many innocent women and children were burnt at the stake. My name is Madelyn Maguire. People call me Maddy and I'm the real McCoy. I'm a full-blown witch. A man by the name of Lucifer has been following me for some time now.

The night it happened.

It was winter. The snow had been falling, leaving a deep blanket of white wool on the ground; nothing could have prepared me for what happened. The fog had gotten thicker by the hour. Looking into the forest, I could feel a distant presence watching me.

"I know you're there Lucifer, come out from behind the trees" I yelled.

He walked from behind the shadows; I looked at him intensely, for I knew what he was. Vampires had been a problem in these parts. I prepared myself, grabbing the wood-cutting ax, I smiled. Approaching me, he seemed different from his usual self.

"I could kill you, Maddy, but there is something about you that intrigues me. In all my years, I have never met someone as powerful and beautiful as you. The things you do, the way you act, pretending you don't love me. I've followed and protected you for years now."

I could have killed him, but I knew it was hopeless. For love had no boundaries, it would travel the earth on the sands of time; it would breathe sexual desire into your body. It would bring two opposites together. Running up to me, I dropped the ax as he kissed me softly on the neck. At that moment, time stood still. I watched as the snowflakes stopped in mid-air in the night's silence. Picking me up, he carried me into the cabin and onto the wooden bed. Tearing my nightdress off with his manly hands, he traveled up my legs, spreading them apart; he went down on me using his tongue to tease me as he slowly worked his way from my ankle kissing his way up to my inner thigh. He kissed his way around my vulva, oh was he getting me to work up and wet. Then he pulled my vulvar inside his mouth and sucked on them, one at a time. Then he began licking my vagina, up and down, slowly. We would occasionally linger at the tip and run his tongue around my clitoris, giving me a tease of what was in store for me, I couldn't wait. I felt his hands on the back of my thighs. He slipped a finger in my vagina while he sucked on my clitoris and teased it with his tongue. Then he slipped another finger through my tight anus and started exploring my rectum. I'd never had both of my holes finger while I was being eaten, it was amazing. He just kept on, sucking and fingering me. It was amazing and oh did me cum hard.

After hugging my thighs and holding me so I could enjoy some post-orgasmic bliss Lucifer put his arms behind my knees and lifted my bum off the bed. He parted my bush and penetrated me with all his hardness. Slowly, he pounded my pussy till I moaned with pleasure. Turning me over, he caressed my soft white breasts from behind and wiggled his shaft inside my pussy again to keep it warm. After massaging my breasts and playing with my nipples he started massing my bum with one hand while his other stayed on my breast. He went after my anal hole with his finger again. He worked my back door for a good long while then he pulled cock out of my pussy and inserted his hardness into the anal hole. I let out a small scream as he pounded my tush over and over. All I could do was grip the bed sheets and moan. Climaxing, he climbed off and slapped my rump.

"Till the next time," he whispered.

A month later, things had heated even more. Lucifer was visiting every night, one night when the stars were glowing and the moon was high in the sky, He finally proposed to me. The ceremony was beautiful. I had worn a long white lace dress dipped in at the waist. Weeks went by and everything was amazing. One morning I woke up to the feeling of nausea in my stomach in the coming weeks I realized I was pregnant.

Telling Lucifer I was pregnant was the happiest I've seen him. I mean, can you imagine a vampire and a witch having a child? 7 months later, I gave birth to a tiny girl we called her was Anna May Maguire. She had the blackest ebony hair and blue eyes. She was born with the skills of a vampire, but with the magic of a witch. She grew fast, too. By the age of 2 weeks, she was a year old.

One bleak morning, I got up and found that she was missing from her bed. She was 7 years old. Hearing screams coming from the local village, I ran as fast as I could. Screaming Anna at the top of my voice.

Getting to the village, I found an intense feeling that something devastating had happened. Lying on the square with their throats ripped out were people from the local village. The more I looked, the more I feared for the worse. Hearing a rustle coming from an alley, I saw Anna eating the remains of a young boy. The flesh was hanging from her mouth. She had gone, full rogue. Her eyes had changed from blue to black. She didn't recognize me as I called her name. Running at me with her fangs out I saw another vampire, with long white hair and wearing a black robe, another original. He gripped her by her neck and lifted her into the air. Screaming, I said,

"No, please don't. She's just a child."

"This is yours. We have rules and you broke them. Who's the father of this thing?" I lied.

"I don't know, he rapped me. I didn't see his face."

This thing will never be a normal child or vampire; it will have no control therefore I'm taking her. She will be brought up by us only. We will teach her to control her bloodlust or she will die." I went running at him but he was gone and so was my beautiful daughter.

Lucifer knew what had happened, as I wept every night. He spent weeks alone. He couldn't look at me without wanting to harm me. He blamed me for not saving her. For letting her out of my sight.

Then one dreadful night he had come home. He was angry. He looked like he had fought with another vampire. I went to ask him how, but he hit me instead. He said everything was falling apart. I took a beating from him every few days till I couldn't take it any longer. Sitting by the burning embers of the fire in my ripped clothes. I knew then I had to kill him, yes he was the one I loved, but the pain and bitterness had changed him and he was the one whom I must kill. Bringing the potions together on a wooden table, I mixed them with precision. Hearing a noise outside, I looked out of the window. He had told the rest of the villagers what I was. They were screaming, "Witch!" I didn't know what to do, so I wrote a quick note saying this is for the Brotherhood of Truth and with that, I cast a homing spell for them to find me. With that, I transported myself into a book.

Gloria's pov

Feeling her in me made me feel different, like small sparks of electricity jolting through my body.

"I will find a way to leave your body, Gloria, but I need time to look for the spell. If you want personal time, let me know?"

I never considered that I looked at Val. He was smirking. He knew what she meant as well. Going back to training, I couldn't help but think about Lucifer and the child. Did he not know where she was? What if she was still alive?

"Madelyn, that's it," I said. "Madelyn, we have to find out for you."

"Then I will need to leave your body as I'm, not my full power staying here. Tell everyone to stand back. I've got the spell"

Floating in the air is amazing. The feeling of being weightless, looking down, and seeing space between your body and the floor, it's all surreal. I could feel her leaving me as I dropped back down to the ground.

"I'm sorry it couldn't have been a longer stay"

We turned to see a woman standing in the room's corner in a blue cotton dress. She was beautiful with her long black locks and blue eyes that sparkled and the fairest of skin. She looked to be about 25 at most. Looking around, she smiled, then approached Sarah and hugged her.

"Thank you for finding me, you, my dear, are special. I hope you have remembered my spells. Now I will share some of my power so you can use them. Don't worry, it won't hurt"

Watching Sarah was amazing. She had this way of sparkling in her way. I could tell by the way Cables watched her as she was blowing vampires apart, she was shining "Fuckkk that's some powerful shit" Cables said.

Laughing was contagious for five whole minutes. We couldn't move.

"I'm going to find my daughter if she is still alive."

Chapter 18

Were we ready to face the originals? Was Madelyn ready to face Lucifer? She had been in the book a few hundred years.

"Madelyn please, you can't face them all," I said.

"What then?" She screamed, "They have my daughter."

"If you join us, you can teach us your ways and we'll teach you how to fight."

After getting Madelyn some proper clothing to fight, i.e. combat trousers were Sarah's thing, not mine; I'm more of the leather trousers look. We headed to the chamber we had converted to practice fighting, by now the other vamps had returned; some were from the local town some were in hiding. Sitting down I watched as Val and

Cables showed them how to fight, turning to see Madelyn but she had gone.

Madelyn's pov

I could off wait, but the thought of my daughter egged me on to leaving Sarah will some spells to practice. I found myself in a quieter area to practice. Taking my necklace with a piece of my daughter's hair, I cast a binding spell on a map Sarah had used. I knew I could tell them what I was doing, but this was something I had to do by myself. I had to mentally connect with Anna. Using an old spell I left my body letting my soul and my mind travel across the waters, to where an ancient church stood with its stained glass windows. Entering the church I noticed it was lit up with flaming candles, the walls were damp yet the place still had an antique feel about it. My mind traveled across the room looking for a way down, there had to be more to see, then I saw it, an old staircase to the left of the corner of the room, I let myself go down the twisting staircase.

I knew she had been here. I sensed her, deeper and deeper as I traveled, below the church, then something unexpected happen, and I saw Lucifer standing in a room with a woman. They were both talking.

"Anna is that you, I whispered in her ear.

Two darting eyes looked straight at me and it wasn't Anna's. I froze as the eyes I recognized was Lucifer's. Did he see me? Did he know I was back inspecting? The girl lifted her head and sniffed

"Mother, is that you?"

Our minds had connected, "Anna, I need you to tell me you are safe."

"Of course, I am with father. He said you were gone and were never coming back. He also said you gave me away."

"Well, I never let you go. They took you from me. Anna believe me"

"Why should she? You left us both, my darling Madelyn."

"Lucifer, how did you find her?"

"It's a long story, but we are together and we will be a family again."

"Don't worry mother, it will be okay."

She sounded off like she was hiding something.

"Not with him never," I replied

"Well then, I will just have to make you..."

With that, I disconnected and re-entered my body, crying I fell to the floor.

"My Anna" I wept.

Anna's pov

When they locked me up I was freighted, yet Gabriel told me he would take care of me as he was my father. Sitting down in a small room with just a single bed and a desk, I couldn't help but think of food and my mother.

"What am I?" looking at him intensely.

"You, my girl, are the first of your kind. You are a part witch and part vampire. If we can control the vampire in you, your witch side can be trained."

I slumped down in my chair.

Everything had changed. My mother was gone and I couldn't see myself ever finding her and my father was here helping me. Sobbing into my pillow, Gabriel sat next to me. Looking into my eyes, he told me to stop crying. Caring me into a larger room, I could see four people standing, shaking.

"Feed then well starts on your training," he said.

He watched as I tore them apart, piece by piece.

Licking the last of the blood from my fingers, I had a strange feeling of this image of a time. Watching, I let the story unfold. I was in a room where two fireside chairs and a boy were sitting at a desk. They were also a larger man with white hair; he was telling the boy off.

"Gabriel, you will do as you're told1"

"But Master Amos, I'm so bored, can't we just visit the local village? We only have to eat one or two people.

"Gabriel, if I let you go to the village, they will start hunting us again. How many times have we moved because of your childish antics? How many innocents will you take? We have an order to stick to," he raised his voice.

Walking off to my room I could see Sebastian training in the dining room. He was 16, I was 13 he was learning how to freeze objects in mid-air, I wanted to be just like him but no I had a job to do, look after stupid vampire brother Lucifer. I hated Lucifer. He was annoying and always seemed to read away the days with his head in the book of the dead. That was when I went to the library. Thousands of books were in large bookcases. I wanted to know more about the humans, what made them tick, how I could get into their heads, how I could control them, and then I could feed without forcing them. I could off asked for help but my brothers were studying their stuff.

Chapter 19

Years later

It was a late night, I had turned 21, and running through the woods with the moon shining on the wet leaves I came across a young boy who had been collecting wood for his cottage. Reading his mind I realized how lonely he was and how hard he worked. I could have killed him but instead, I watched him grow up. As the years passed on, Lucifer asked me questions about who the boy was. One frosty night after Lucifer disappeared, I found him eating the remains of the boy. That night, I beat Lucifer to a pulp. I told him I would have revenge for what he did, yes I was a vampire, but the more I knew about my food, the better I could control them.

Anna's pov

Lucifer killed the boy, but what Gabriel didn't know was that the boy had a sister, an exquisite girl named Madelyn. Born out of wedlock, the baby girl was cast out in a basket. Traveling down the river, she landed on a tuft of grass-like magic itself that had taken her there. Winter was a hard time, but spring was coming, the river was running, and the daffodils had opened their heads.

Clare Maguire was collecting herbs when she heard a faint cry coming from a nearby riverbank. Upon investigating Clara found the baby wrapped up in a tartan blanket, looking at the baby's blue eyes, Clara fell deeply in love with the child realizing how special the girl was and how powerful she would become.

The year was 1830

The snow had fallen on the Scottish mountain of Lochness leaving nothing but a crisp layer of softness. Taking the baby, she took her home. Clara practiced her magic whilst Madelyn watched.

"It will be spring here soon my gal, I can feel it in my bones, my love. Madelyn, get them wee herbs from the glass over here. I have to make this potion better, so we can put up an extra barrier to keep the heat in. As the years went by and the winters passed, so did Madelyn's powers come to the surface. She needed no herbs or potions. She was born with special energy, a blue light that gave her body a white glow, only when angry would the light combust spreading for miles.

Madelyn's and Lucifer's love

I could smell him from miles away. He gave a potent smell of old blood, but he had the most beautiful of brown eyes and a smile that could soften even the hardest madam.

"You can come out. I can smell you."

Coming from behind, he gripped me around my neck. Kissing him, we fell to the ground, giggling.

"Why can't I kill you? You drive me nuts Madelyn, you are all I think about. I'm sure you put a witch spell on me."

"A spell? I don't need any portions for that Lucifer. You've watched me for how long now? You know what I am, you always have. Magic is part of me, and me it."

That night we spent lying on the wet snow making snow angels. We were young. We had the entire world to see.

Lucifer's love

Watching her in her blue dress as she picked berries in the moonlight had me wanting to hold her. What had she done to me? What magic had she used on me? This is the first time I didn't want to eat anyone. Sitting down on a log to think, I noticed she had appeared next to me.

"So, you're a vampire of the night. How's it going for you?"

Looking at her, I couldn't quite think straight. Her blue eyes sparkled in the darkness.

"I guess it's all right, it could be worse than being a vampire, I could be dead."

She burst out laughing.

"I'm Lucifer I said and you."

"I'm Madelyn Maguire of the Lochness hills."

She smiled. As the year passed, I grew more in love with her, and as the years passed, I followed her as she traveled the world. But the year our daughter Anna was born was amazing. She was the first of her kind, but she grew so fast that the night my daughter was taken I had an intense feeling of anger blaming Madelyn. I found I couldn't control the anger within me and I found myself using blunt force on her, watching myself hit her. I left and headed to the local tavern, rum was my go-to drink in a panic.

Anna's pov

I couldn't help but freeze for a moment. I had just witnessed my mother and Lucifer together and it wasn't Gabriel, my father. What was going on here? I had just witnessed Lucifer hitting my mother. Turning to face Gabriel, I wanted to ask, but instead, I looked at him most disgustingly. That was the last night I would remain a child. That night I sat in my room using my power to grow up and I knew I was about to let myself free. I wanted my mother. My father never knew how much of my mother's power was within me. I would bid my time and then leave.

Gloria's pov

As I watched everyone training, I couldn't help but think about the cage with all the children in it. I wondered if they knew what they were. Looking at Val, I thought he wouldn't notice me slip out into the darkness. There were things I just couldn't leave. Considering my options, I made my way to my bike.

"Don't stop me," I said as I turned to see Val. He gripped me around the waist and kissed me.

"I wasn't, but next time at least tells me I do worry about you. So what's going on in that pretty mind or yours? Where are we heading?"

He already knew where I was heading. He was just being sarcastic.

"Come on," I said, nudging him.

"What, on that thing?" he said.

"Don't call her that, her name is Harley. She's the best motorbike going, and she gives one hell of a ride."

Okay, I'll meet you there."

As I climbed on my bike, he left. The ride was great, with the wind in my hair and no one to bother me. Reaching the tunnels, I saw Val waiting for me. I just needed to know the truth. We walked down the tunnels and came to the hole.

"See you down there," I said, smiling.

Reaching the bottom made me giggle.

"Do you remember the last time?"

"Yeah, it was a ravishing moment"

We were about to pounce on each other and repeat the action when something caught our attention. Hearing a few men talking perked our interest. Walking deeper into the tunnel, we got closer to military men. I hated them two-faced, ass-kissing vamps; we watched and waited in the shadows.

"Dinner," I said, turning to my husband. He grinned at me.

"You first, my darling."

Jumping from mid-air I sank my teeth into the 1st man's neck, he let out a scream As I drained him of his lovely blood I couldn't help but giggle, I was in bloody heaven. I turned to see Val ripping a leg off his leftover copse. Knelling down, I searched the pockets of my copse, pulling out a card. It read Scablands Industries, two and two started to add together. Cables' father was the head of this company and the military was defiantly working for him. Fuck, I hated him.

Leaving nothing but a few bones, we came to the room where the shapeshifters were kept. The cages were near enough empty except for a pile of puttied decaying skin. We needed to find them. Sniffing the air, we both nodded to each other. We knew where there were and we knew where they were heading.

Chapter 20

The underground sewage pipes were where we had to go. Climbing back on my bike, I told Val I would meet him there, kissing him I left.

The ripening smell of death was in the air. Pulling out my swords, I smiled like the Cheesier bloody Cat. Val told me to be careful as he went down one of the sewage tunnels always staying in contact mentally. I was lucky I could see through the darkness following the stench of dead bodies. I walked on through the sludge of shit and water. Coming to a ladder, I climbed up. Using force, I opened the manhole cover. Fuck shit, I couldn't quite believe what I was seeing. A large compound that was separated into different compartments reminded me of a Roman arena where the gladiators fought.

"Val, can you see this? There's a hundred of them."

Scarps were lined up by the hundreds. If we were to do something, we would have to do it now.

"Val, honey, we have to burn them all. If they get out into the streets, they will kill even the lowest of vamps, let alone take our food source."

We would never kill an innocent, though. Transforming Val stared at me with a grin as my skin peeled away and my back arched and cracked, watching my hands turn to long legs and my nails turn to claws left me with a wow feeling I was tremendous.

Stretching my long veiny black wigs, I growled "freedom at last". Fire blasted out of my mouth as I let out a snort of steam.

"Are you ready, my love?" Val said.

I looked at his transformed body and nodded.

Lighting up thousands of scarps in the night left me with a saddened feeling as to what they once were. Could I have killed them if they were still children? I shook the thought out of my head and carried on. Scarps were screaming and dropping down to the ground as we killed them, even the odd one that had tried to escape we had to kill. Transforming back into ourselves, we stood there watching as the fires blazed in the night. Leaving, I gripped Val's hand as I knew it was just the beginning.

Going back to Cables and Sarah we both sank into the chairs by the fire, it felt so good to be able to rest. Then I heard her "Gloria I need to see you," it was Mercy, standing up I walked over to the door, there's no peace for the dead I thought. As I walked through the enormous doors, I turned to see Val coming behind.

Stay in the shadows, my love, just listens. Mercy was standing in the alley across the road. Gloria, my child, we have to be quick.

"Lucifer has found out about you. He is really mad that I kept you a secret."

I noticed a cut across her face that had started to heal.

"Lucifer needs to die," I said. I heard Madelyn say:

"You don't have to worry. I've got this."

Did everyone follow me? I was right they had. Going to turn to Madelyn was pointless for she had gone. Cables and Sarah walked out of the darkness.

"Can anyone sense her?"

"She used her magic, my love, to put a blocking spell on us. Whatever she's doing, she's got a plan. It will take Sarah a while to find an unblocking spell."

"Wait Mercy, take me now." She went to say no, but I growled at her, I wasn't asking. I demanded that we transform into a mist and left.

Madelyn's pov

Transporting onto the grounds of an old boarding school had me wondering about Anna. Was she here and would she know how to use her magic? Making myself invisible I walked through the corridors sending out a blue light spell I asked the light to find Anna. The light led me to a small room, far away at the end of the corridor. Peeking through the door I saw not a child but a woman, with blue eyes reading a book she quickly turned her head.

"Mother, is that you? Don't worry, he's busy, but he won't be long. We need to be quick." Making myself visible, the woman jumped up and wrapped her arms around me.

"It's been so long, my daughter."

"Quick, come on let's go."

"Wait Anna," I said.

"I have something to do the first Mother. I knew how to use our magic, so I want you and myself together to cast an illusion spell. It has to be long enough for my father to think it's real, if we can trap him he will relive the same moment over and over without realizing we have left."

"I have just the memories we can use, the day you were born," I said to Anna. Joining hands, we both concentrated. The light in our eyes lit up, and the magic set an illusion just for him.

"Now let's go," I said.

Turning myself and Anna invisible, we ran just as Lucifer returned from his misdeeds. Running past the doors and out of the building, we ran across the grass with our hearts beating fast. If it wasn't for Gloria tracking me with the help of Mercy, we wouldn't have gotten away. Hearing a man's screams echo across the waters left me feeling uneasy. Luckily Gloria had offered us a faster way to travel [by mist], Mercy had already returned to the school to cover her own back I guess.

Taking Anna back to the underground station, we went into the carriage. Val and Gloria had gone for some alone time and Cables and Sarah were rambling on about fighting and what weapons to use in the coming war. Sitting down, I couldn't help but cry.

"We have to put a blocking spell up so he can't find us or enter the station."

Drawing a circle, we got the candles set out and ready.

"A circle we draw and a spell we have cast to protect us from Lucifer and the darkness he is."

Together, a blinding blue light lit up and left the circle.

"Right, now that the shield is done. Know it's time we learn the darkest of the spells."

Sarah joined us. Watching Sarah and Anna join forces made me feel proud to be a witch.

Cables' pov

I couldn't believe I was training vamps to fight; I held back my lust to eat them and focused on teaching them to hit hard and flash. A small girl vamp had to be my favorite, for she was like a quarterback that could run as fast as the wind with two small knives. She was dangerous; she practiced on a dummy we'd made up from old sandbags.

Watching vamps flip each other led me to think about the weapons we had used. I had been talking it through with Sarah, we had to be prepared, who knew what the others had or would use. Throwing a knife I hit the dummy right in the head what, I needed to do was move faster whilst transforming. Looking at everyone, I gave them notice so to speak as to what I was. Transforming, I ran at the dummies, but the vamps were making it more of a duck and miss as they chucked them at me, all of them falling to the floor. In the end, they clapped. Now it was their turn. I had to teach them to transform at first the larger vamps changed into a small pack of wild boar. Then it was the young girl with red hair, watching her concentrate I watched as her body changed into a red fox, only appropriate to what she was I thought. We all sat down to drink our blood, supplied by yours truly i.e. the fridge at Gloria's place. We sat quiet, just relaxing. I was thinking of getting Gloria, but I thought against it. The two were seriously in love and I wasn't to be the one to catch them at it. So I stayed put.

Gloria's pov

It might have been easier to just get our kits off, but we wanted to take our time. We had hundreds of years to catch up on, so instead of just ripping our clothes off and fucking, we took our time. Undressing him slowly each button of his once white shirt flipped open, kissing his chest slowly, he followed suit lifting my black tank top over my head leaving me with just my red bra. Removing it slowly he caressed my cleavage with his manly hands leaving me gasping with erotic pleasure.

Biting my neck, he sucked my blood, leaving me wanting more. I couldn't take this slow shit anymore, I was thinking. Ripping his trousers off, I grabbed his hard cock in my hands. He gasped with delight as I took it in my mouth. I felt his hands clench as I let my lips do the work and my tongue tease him. After a few seconds, he picked me up, and we landed up against a tunnel wall. Lifting me onto his hard cock he pushed himself inside me harder and harder; I let out a scream of delight the rougher it got.

The pain was a sexual pleasure now. Kissing me passionately we slid down the wall for the roughness to increase biting him and then letting him rub the blood into my body sent me crazy with passion, his fingers trailed to my pussy I groaned in pleasure as he fingered me with delight, again and again, I moaned leaving an echo to travel down the tunnel. I couldn't stop myself at that moment; I climbed onto his hard cock and rode him into the fucking night. Climaxing, we both lay there in the darkness; he looked at me with an enormous smile.

Walking back to the others, I wondered what Cables' father was doing, knowing we had burnt his little army of sarbs.

Cables' father's pov

It was late when one of my headmen came running in. Looking at him, I knew something was wrong.

"What!" I demanded.

"Boss, it's the compound, they are all dead, just burning embers remain not one scarp is left."

"What the fuck? Get me my car." I yelled across the room.

Walking to my car, which was waiting for me, I couldn't quite understand what I had done to deserve all this mayhem, but I knew one thing: Gloria and her group of merry men were dead. By the time I had got to the compound, it was midnight. I couldn't take in all the destruction, the fires were blazing, and buildings were set alight, but to see my babies as ashes on the ground made me furious, this was war by any means. Leaving, I ordered my men to fetch the other head vamps. We were having a meeting, whether they liked it or not.

Waiting in my conference room, I paced up and down.

"You shouldn't have underestimated Gloria and her little gang, you know. I found some useful information about our little Gloria. Let's say there's more to her than we knew, our little Gloria has a history. She was brought up by one of us 200 years ago I think that's right by my working out when she was reborn."

"Who bought her up? Maybe we can use them against her."

"Bring her in boys"

I watched as they dragged a woman in. She was tall but exquisite with her long black hair. Looking at her, I realized that Gloria was her daughter. Shaking my head, I grinned. "Take her to the cell. I'll be there soon."

The Meeting

It was 2 am by the time they arrived. Five head vamps from five different districts, I noticed a couple had not bothered turning up, wankers, I thought.

"I call this meeting regarding a certain lady and her merry clan of men. Gloria Snips and her beloved husband, the one and only Count Dracula. For many months she and her merry men have been bloody flees under my armpit, scratching away at every chance they can. They have stood in our way of having full domination. Only this evening did they kill a thousand of my pet scarps. This woman is an abomination to us all, she must pay for her misdeeds, plus to make matters worse she has kidnapped my one and only son, Cables. I have considered our options and I declare by territory rights to use an army of vamps to take them down."

Waiting for the response, I paced up and down. They all started mumbling between each other.

"We have a group agree, said Darken Trent. War is the only course we can take against this woman and her friends. We will prepare our troops of vampires. We wish you a good night. As they left, I decided to go to the cell, even though Lucifer would disagree, but he wasn't here anymore to disagree.

Walking to the cell, all I could think about was the woman, opening the cell door I walked in.

"What's your name?"

"They call me Mercy. Why am I locked away like this? I am an original; I could break your neck with just a thought."

Circling her, I admired her long neck and her pale skin with her long black hair. I was seriously crushing on her, yes I'm a monster, but we still have our needs. Lucifer would kill me if he knew what I was about to do. Leaning forward, I braced myself and went in for a kiss. Expecting her to be repulsed, but it was the complete opposite. She kissed me back, and that blew my mind. What followed was pure and utter love-making at its finest. Her skin is a lovely pale, with the blackest of hair, such a beautiful and sexy combination. She was so easy on the eyes. It was so hot to slowly undress her, one item at a time until she was standing there naked in front of me, in all her glory. I helped her lay down and worked my way up her soft, sensuous leg. When I got to my groin her thick black hair hid the treasure I was seeking. The bright pink of her vagina complemented her black hair and lily-white skin. And oh my word did her pussy taste amazing. After her orgasm, I climbed my way up and mounted my new lady. Oh, it felt so go to penetrate her body and just savor the feeling of her moist vagina wrapped around my penis. Feeling her voluptuous breasts against my bare chest as I thrust in and out of her and we ground our pelvises was awesome. I kept the pace slow so I could keep kissing her as we explored each other's mouths with our tongues. Gazing at her elegant face I was captivated, I couldn't wait to watch her face and see her expressions when she orgasmic again, and I wasn't disappointed. It was amazing to finish inside her and get her all gooey and messy. I rolled off her to the side and pulled her with me. Laying there face to face with our legs all tangled up and rubbing each other's back made me feel wanted, even though I had left myself wide open to her charms.

Mercy's pov

Always have a plan

As we walked into this tiny room they call a cell, I couldn't help but see Cables' asshole of a father giving a long-winded speech about Gloria feeling lost. I knew what I had to do. One thing I had known over the years was to use my feminine charms for the good. Opening a small bottle, filled with an extremely potent pheromone I let the yellow mist drift down the corridor of the dome. Focusing all along on Cable's father, having sex with a monster like him, I just had to forget what he was and let my feminine wilds take over. Whilst I lay there naked in his arms I connected to Gloria. "My daughter, I have been captured by a very greedy man who wishes harm on you and your friends, I need you to get ready for the time is coming, don't worry about me I have my ways of escaping. I will join you soon as I can" with that we parted our connection.

I was just lying there; I spread my legs to lure him in. I can't describe how bored I was. I was just letting him use my vagina to masturbate, hoping that if I was loose with my [pussy he would be loose in the lips and I could get some Intel. Jess, when you want a guy to bust a nut in record time suddenly he's a long-distance runner. Come on already, blow your disgusting wad in my twat, and be done with it. I couldn't wait to wash up afterward.

At times it's handy being a woman. I can lie here, letting my mind wander to distract me from the disgusting monster bouncing up and down on top of me. He thinks I'm all hot, Horney, and lusting for him. He has no clue I'm faking the entire thing, I deserve an Oscar for this performance. Whereas it's REALLY difficult for a guy to fake things.

Chapter 21

Gloria's pov

Listening to my mother tell me what was going on I knew I had to tell the others sitting in the old train carriage, I shared my worries.

"They will try to come for us all, and you know what? Not on my fucking watch! I'm done hiding. Cables. Your father is out of control. There's only one way this is going to end."

"I agree, I've tried so hard to love him but he makes it impossible for me to even change his mind, he wants full control and anyone who fights him will pay." Cables replied. Hearing a yell from Anna, we went to see what had happened.

"It's Sarah; she was practicing a dark magic spell whilst my mother was praying when she went rogue on us. I went to stop her, but she vanished just like that."

"Vanished where?"

"She was mumbling about going to end the reign of Lucifer, once and for all, and her eyes."

"What about her eyes?"

"They are as black as a demon; my mother's looking for a spell to contact her."

Cables looked terrified before his vamp bear took over and the bear itself came to play.

Cables' pov

Hearing that my girl had gone missing sent me nuts. I was done waiting. Running out of the underground train station, I let out a roar. Heading to my father's facility, I felt someone was running alongside me. Turning to see Val beside me, I smiled. We ran through the doors like a fucking whirlwind. Gripping vamps and tearing them apart piece by piece. Seeing my father sitting by the fire reading, I walked straight on in there.

"Where is he?"

"Whom are you talking about?"

"Lucifer and the other fucking originals"

My father looked scared. He had never witnessed me go, full rogue; he stood up and backed off. I was so sick of his bullshit antics, arranging wars, and cloning everything and everyone. Reading his mind, I sensed where the originals were. I went to leave, but he caught my arm.

"You are not to get involved, I warned you before."

That was that I turned, picked him up by his neck, and said,

"I will never listen to you again. They are my friends you are fighting with and if you don't stop this war, I will. Do you understand?"

I growled. I let him go, and he went running, but Val had already caught him.

"Don't bother chasing him," Val said. "He's just a clone."

"Fuck!" I screamed.

"Come on, we have to get to the old boarding school on the opposite side of the water. Sarah's over there."

Traveling by mist was quite an experience. We demised by the entrance. Val sniffed the air. "She's here, but I can't connect mentally. Come on, she was this way."

Walking through the dark corridors, we came to a room. "What the fuck is happening here Val?"

It was like watching something from the twilight zone. She had created not only a black hole, but a fucking portal to another dimension. Shouting, "Sarah", all I got was an echo. "Fuck it, I'm going in."

"Wait," Val said.

"I see something, someone's coming through" replied Val, and by someone I mean a fucking army, and Sarah's leading them. Watching them march through, was nothing but magical. Sarah walked up to me and her black eyes flicked back to their usual blue.

"Cables, I'm here. Yeah, maybe I've gone to the dark side, she laughed. But fucking Lucifer, that cock sucking mother fucker, asked for it!" She gave me a quick kiss, we both wanted more, but that would have to wait.

"Babes, now calm down and tell me what's happening."

"Let's get out of here first," Sarah replied.

"What's with the army?"

These are Margo's family. Each one is the head of an ancient witch community. Each one has drawn in enough power from their worldly dimensions to kill every Lucifer in every fucking world. This is war.

"Where's Lucifer?"

"He bolted when he saw Margo. He had her cast away into the darkness for she was becoming more powerful than he ever was."

"Who's Margo?" Val said listening.

"Margo is the most powerful, darkest witch ever to walk the earth. I found her when I accidentally opened the *Book of the Dead*. We connected. She will remain within me till the war has ended."

"Come on, let's get back." I was worried sick about the fact that she carried someone else inside her. I also wondered who might be inside her when we've had sex. Are they able to read my mind while Sarah is fucking me? Can they do it if we're only kissing?

"Don't worry, I promise not to hurt her." I heard a woman say.

By the time we got back, Gloria had already introduced herself to all the women. How did she do that I thought? I must remember to ask her. They all took to the tunnels, gassing about magic. All I could do was sit down on a chair on the cartridge and worry. Madelyn and Anna had already made friends. Sarah followed me, standing against the desk.

"So what happens now?" Val said.

"We train," said Gloria.

Madelyn's pov

Walking into the room, I noticed something very familiar about Sarah's body, sniffing her I smiled. The scent of wildflowers then hit me.

"Margo, is that you in there?"

Sarah turned around and smiled as her eyes flicked to black color.

"Finally, you are back. Do you know how long I have waited to see you?" said Madelyn.

"Madelyn, my little sister, how I've missed you. Come here and hug your big sister."

"Margo, he hurt me so badly, he took my daughter."

"I know, I tried to help you, I tried to get the revenge. He had me bloody locked away in another dimension. But now I'm stronger, I have a better vessel and an army. We will take him down, I promise."

Gloria's pov

Well, I couldn't help but clap, what an outcome.

"You pair are sisters."

I said, pointing.

"So what happened at the boarding school?"

I said randomly to Sarah.

Sarah's eyes flicked back.

"He fucking ran, that's what. He knows she's back, and he's going to try to hide," Sarah's eyes flicked back.

I'm going to tell you a tale from a long time ago, about two sister witches that had their lives ruined by the likes of the originals. We were brought up in the Lochness Mountains. Life was hard, but we were happy. Living in the caves, we had everything we needed till my sister met him. Madelyn was so happy, she told us about a man she had fallen for. One night, I couldn't help but follow her. I stayed back to watch. As she laughed with him I noticed who he was. It was Lucifer. I didn't want to tell her that I had already seen him. I should have killed him that night when I saw what he did to a young boy from the shack in the woods. He was a fucking cold-blooded vampire, and she was dating him. Me being an idiot, I let her carry on seeing him. And when they married and had Anna, I watched from the darkness when I found out he had hurt her. I ragged a personal war against him, but he hired a group of rogues to attack me. I killed a few, but they caught me. Using a spell from my book, he summoned a bounty hunter named Drager, who dragged me through a portal. The only way back to your world was through a back door, and with that, I attached my consciousness to the B*ook of the Dead*. When Sarah read the book, it was my only chance, if I could have found another way I would of. I promise I won't hurt her, but when Lucifer is dead to me and Cable's father's army is defeated, I will find a way to exist outside of the book and outside of another."

Cables' pov

Did I trust her? No, but I had no choice. Sarah seemed stronger than ever as I sat here listening to Margo's story.

"So, where is your body?" I said.

Margo turned and looked at me. "Gone when Drager took me to his world, I was taken to a cell and starved to death. During my last few days, it took everything I had to transfer myself."

So what happens after the vampire army has been defeated? Where will you go?"

"With I," said, Madelyn.

"We are sisters and we are meant to be but we can only use one set of powers per vessel, That's why she is staying with Sarah until it ended" After we will open a portal and go back in time to when we were happy and we will make it different"

Val's pov

Gripping Gloria's hand I pulled her to walk with me, I had something to say. "Gloria, my love, after it is over we are going back. We'll take Oliver and head for our home in Transylvania. The manor house is still standing; I paid a lot of money to keep it going so we can start again."

"Val, I would love that," I said as we walked back.

Gloria's pov

I needed to ride; I needed to feel the wind in my hair. I couldn't believe we were going to war. Why couldn't Cables' father just be normal? Why did he have to want to walk in the daylight? Touching my necklace I knew what I had to do. After telling Val I was going for a ride to clear my head I left. I could have headed for the open roads, but I headed to the city where the street gangs hanged out. Pulling over, I climbed off my bike and headed for the left side of the city. Seeing a small group of humans standing about a burning oil can, I took to speaking with them. First, they looked scared, but after I told them I wouldn't eat them they took me to meet the head of their so-called clan. It surprised me as the clan leader was a woman, show must have been in her late 30s with brown curly hair, kitted out in full leathers. Taking a seat, I told her what was going to happen in the coming nights. I also told her if she wanted to join in the fights, she was more than welcome to. She looked shocked at first, but the thought of having revenge on the vamps was quite inviting. Leaving her with her thoughts, I left. I climbed back on my bike and rode. Cables' father's army was on my mind, playing like a fucking record player. I knew then what I needed to do.

"Mercy, are you there?" I said.

"Hello my daughter, I see you have been busy."

"Yes, mother but I need to know how many vamps are against us."

"Wait, I will try to see using what magic I have. I will get back to you as soon as I can."

Riding, I left my thoughts behind me.

Chapter 22

No surrender, no mercy

Mercy's pov

Sitting in my cell, I decided it was time to play the damsel in distress. I had to get out of this shit hole of a cell. Calling for the guard, who was wandering up and down like a prison guard on night shift? I asked to speak to Cable's father. I didn't know his name, so I gave him the name dick face as that was what he looked like. Dickey boy came strolling down the corridor.

"Oh, my darling. I'm so uncomfortable isn't there a way I can get a better cell or maybe share your bed," I said pretending to sob.

He paced up and down and put his hands on his hips.

"Arrrh, fuck Lucifer. He isn't the one that's getting his cock sucked for free. Come on, you can stay with me."

Smiling to myself, we walked on through some very large wooden doors to an elegant room. There was a large wooden bed with an animal's head above it, looked like a lion. Bastard, I thought. Sitting down, he offered me a small drink of A-Negative blood.

"Well, that's a rare find, to have fresh blood," I said.

"My love, we have all the latest blood pumps available. We only use the best of the breed from the best of the crop, so to speak."

Having sex with him was boring but amusing as he pumped away with his small pencil he called a dick. One thing's for sure, I won't be sore tomorrow. Fortunately, he was quick; I'm guessing it's been a while since he's poked a live woman. I could feel the weight of his body on top of me but I barely felt anything inside of me. How hum, the things I do.

I'd always been a keen reader of the requirements of learning magic. Using a minor spell, I put him into a deep sleep. The end justifies the means so I had to let him have a quick go at my pussy to get out of that cell, but let's not be crazy about things.

Going over to his old antique cabinet, I opened the top drawer.

"Hum let me see," I said to myself.

Picking up a document that said confidential, I started to read, well I'll be, he wasn't just building an army of vamps he was building a new facility in the north. I carried on reading through the papers there were details of all the clones they had made. From the rich businessman to your famous singers, even the fucking president was on the list. In my thousands of years of being dead, I have never seen such a fucked up society, this world had gone to shit.

Walking over to Cables' so-called father who lay in a deep sleep, I leaned over and covered his mouth and bit his neck. His eyes widened, and I knew from that taste he was just another body to turn into dust. "Fucking clones!" I spat on the floor. Grabbing the papers, I let myself turn into a dark mist and traveled as far as I could, out of reach of Lucifer's claws, so I could read more.

Sitting on an old tree stump in the deepest part of the forest, I looked closely at the list of clone names and the prices they paid. I knew I had to see if Gloria and the others taking a risk that was worth it for my daughter's sake.

"Gloria, I need to meet you and the others as soon as possible. Can you hear me?"

Gloria's pov

Reaching the abandoned train station, I walked down the steps, into the old cartridge, and slumped in the chair. Val was gazing at me.

"What?"

"Nothing just worried about you. We are a team, you know."

Sitting there staring into space, I heard my mother. She was eager to meet us and had some news.

"Val, we have to go. Cables make sure we are not followed. Margo, can you keep the barrier up?"

"Yes," she said. Leaving, I gripped Val and kissed him.

"Just in case anything should happen to us."

"I feel like flying tonight darling," I said as I looked at Val.

Transforming into Dragons we took to the sky. Opening our wings, we soared through the air, landing on a patch of grass near where my mother was sitting patiently.

"Hi mother"

"Nice landing. Hello Gloria and Val, please let's walk."

She was wearing a long black cloak with red satin embroidery.

"So, what's wrong?"

"I need you both to see this."

Receiving the papers, I scanned through them, each one I then passed to Val. I couldn't take it in, but I knew one thing: I was taking it all down, no more clones. I'm guessing when the shit went down; the rich didn't want to become chowder for the vamps, so they paid the military to put them into Statius. Whilst their clones ran around causing no end of trouble. So did Cables' father knows what his clones were doing? I'm sure as hell he did. I mean, it was still his brain that was working away. That gave me an idea. It was quite evil, in fact.

"What if we destroy the facility where the clones are being made? Wouldn't that give us leverage on who is who?"

"Mother, I need you to get out of here and find a way to keep safe. When this shit hits the fan, all hell will break loose. I'm going to end this once and for all."

"We need to get the others," Val replied.

My mother kissed us goodbye and misted away. Plus, I'm sure she had her stuff to deal with. We went back to the underground station and called for everyone and I mean everyone to come for a meeting. Telling them all what the confidential papers read, we drew up a plan of action.

With the changing of the times and the streets being deserted, we all have our agenda to want to kill. Some do it for food, and some do it out of pure jealousy. Me, I do it because I believe in the good out ways the bad. Talking to Margo and the other witches, I realized they wanted to face Lucifer first. Revenge is evil, but a must at times. No surrender, no mercy — that was their motto. I had heard that so many times growing up. It had become second nature. Everyone wanted revenge on someone.

Whilst the witches headed to fight Lucifer. We would head for the facility in the northern flank of the district. Cables' hands were tied. He had to make a choice on whom to join and he was with Sarah. Looking at Val, I smiled devilishly.

"Time to bust some ass."

Everyone was running around, grabbing weapons and ammo. All I wanted was my two babies, my swords of hell.

"Wait!" said Sarah, running. "I made a few changes to your coat."

Picking up my leather trench coat, she showed me what she had done.

"I've put poisoned knife tips in the bottom. All to have to do is press this button on the sleeve of your coat and the knives come out. Let me show you."

"It was really quite amazing that Margo has made you this," said Val. I watched as she passed him a bracelet of gold. "All you've got to do is press the clear diamond in the middle. It's a time portal. It'll take you back to wherever you want to be, and also I want to give you this. Passing him a small bottle, "it's a healing juice Val; you know what it's for." Sarah looked at me and smiled.

"See you when I can. I love you both." With that, they left.

"Looks like it's up to us to lead the way my love"

Would Margo and the others be okay? I hoped she would take care of Sarah.

Chapter 23

Sarah's pov

Witches of all different dimensions came with Margo; each had created a portal key, and each had a reason to fight. Sending out a spell to find Lucifer was just the beginning. We needed to get him to come and stand on holy ground.

The Charters Church Graveyard had been abandoned for almost 500 years. Old gravestones had stood the test of time and green moss grew up the walls of the old buildings. Margo took to the front of the group, stood on a platform of stones, and gave a speech.

"Ladies, I stand here now with my sisters. We are to call upon our dead ancestors to join us in this war against Lucifer. For far too long Lucifer has traveled to our worlds and destroyed what we stand for, and we will have our revenge. We will force him out of the darkness.

"How?" shouted one witch.

"We'll use his daughter, Anna"

"Mother, let her. He does love me."

"I won't let you, Margo, she's all I have," said Madelyn.

"Seriously, are you taking a stance against me?"

"I have an idea," said one of the older witches at the front.

"Well, we'll use an illusion spell. He'll think that it's her."

"Okay Anna, we need you to pretend you're in danger. Can you do that?" said Margo.

"Yes," she replied, "then he will come."

Lucifer's pov

Coming back to the school, I noticed a few things. First, I went to see Gabriel's daughter check if she was okay. I always found her remarkably talented, and she had the bluest of eyes. But all I found was an empty room. I went to turn, but Gabriel stood in the doorway with his arms crossed. "She's gone. And there is something I need to tell you, come with me. Let's sit in the dining room, my brother" Lucifer took to a seat.

"Do you remember the boy from the forest?"

"Yes, he tasted very nice. Why?"

"Well, guess what he was. He was mine, I had watched him as a small boy and you killed him,"

"He was just a human, don't be too mellow dramatic," Lucifer replied.

Dramatic, well here's one for you. It was me who took your lovely daughter and treated her as my own. I blocked her memory of ever knowing you."

Well, fuck me, did I lose it? I ran and punched him in the face. He grinned spitting blood on the ground.

"Is that all you've got brother?" Gabriel shouted.

Pouncing through the air, I went to grab him. Gabriel gave me a sharp uppercut to the chin sending me flying, across the living room floor.

"You're just a bastard," I said as I clambered back onto my feet.

"She's my daughter, and she's been under my nose all this time. I thought my daughter was dead "

"Well, you'll know for the next time not to take something that is not your brother."

With that, I turned into a Black Dragon and so did he. Smashing through the ceiling of the school wasn't my intention, but killing my brother was. I was going to rip him apart. Busting through the ceiling, I let Gabriel have a full-blown fireball. Gabriel snorted whilst he put up his wing to block the fireball from hitting him.

"So you want to play dirty brother?" he laughed.

"Take this" a double ball of fire came at me.

Flying higher, I stopped in mid-air.

"Gabriel stop, listen."

We could hear Anna sobbing. Landing back on the ground, we menacingly stared at each other.

"Till later I growled, "I'm going to get my daughter."

"Not without me, she's still my daughter as far as I'm concerned Lucifer"

The cheeky fucker, I thought, as we left to find Anna.

Anna's pov

Thinking back to the memories of my mother and that day I saw Lucifer attack my mother, made me feel lost. I couldn't believe he was my father and a horrible one at that. Fuck him I thought, but what about Gabriel, he had been there all these years.

"Mother, I need to talk to you."

My mother had been through hell, but she still hid from my father and she didn't try to find me. I was so confused

"Anna, what's wrong?"

I was so bloody annoyed; I knew I should have asked her before.

"Why did you not bother looking for me over the past 200 years? Why did you let me think you were dead all these years?"

Walking over to me, she put her arms around me as if it was okay.

"Mother!"

I yelled, startling all the other witches.

"You left me mother and you let him hit you. Why? You are the sister of the most powerful witch on earth. Why didn't you go to her?"

"Stop it," I heard Margo's voice.

"Leave the past where it is"

Staring, I stormed off and found myself a stone to sit on.

"You shouldn't believe any of them."

I heard a male's voice say.

"Who are you to tell me what to believe?"

"I'm the one that searched the earth for you. You were a child; you didn't have to grow up so fast. How did I know that my beautiful niece was my daughter? Gabriel lied to me and you for all these years. Cutting him off was all that I could do. I needed time to think.

Margo's pov

I was watching Anna when I heard her shout.

"He's here" I screamed, ladies are you ready" Lifting my head to see a terrifying dragon set fire to the ground below. Turning, I noticed Anna was gone.

"Lucifer shows you. I want to see the real you, are you scared to face me?"

Watching the flames burn the ground alight. I watched as the rest of the witches lay dead on the ground. How I thought?

"My brother darling" I heard Lucifer say as he walked towards me.

"Margo, how long has it been? I see you have bought my brother some snacks," he said, laughing. Scanning the area I feared for the worse, and then I saw something rather unusual: a bear was running towards Lucifer with teeth and all; I could hear Sarah screaming in my head:

"Let me out!" with that I let her out.

Sarah's pov

Watching Cables run at Lucifer made my heart sink. I couldn't let him sacrifice himself for us; I ran towards them and watched as Cables hit Lucifer full-on. For a whole ten minutes, it was like slow, bloody motion.

"Margo, help him," I screamed.

Putting her hand up she sent out a lightning bolt to hit Lucifer, but Lucifer was too fast, within seconds he had moved and the bolt of lightning had caught Cables instead. Watching him hit the ground left me with a fear of God inside me and I feared for the worse.

Margo's pov

"Listening to Sarah cry broke my heart, but I didn't stop. I kept throwing lightning bolts, hoping to hit Lucifer."

"Stop or ill snap her neck." I heard a man say.

Turning around, I saw another vampire gripping my sister by her neck

Anna's pov

I couldn't take it anymore. My whole family was fighting over me; Running out with a knife was all that I could do.

"No father, please!"

I said as I walked from behind a building. My eyes felt like fire. They were burning like hell from crying.

"Father, this is between us five. Margo, back off, please. I'm sick of the arguments. If you don't stop fighting, I'll kill myself." I was aiming a knife at my stomach.

"We need to talk as a family and that means you to Lucifer."

Margo froze, and so did the rest of my family. She and my mother didn't expect me to jump in, and neither did my fathers.

"Margo, let it go. She's right. We are all family and revenge will never solve our problems."

I heard my mother say:

"My father, Gabriel, let her go" and we all walked together. Watching the way Lucifer and my mother looked at each made me realize that there was still a lot of love there, despite the fighting.

"Wait a min," Margo said. "I have one thing to do." Looked at my mother. I saw her spirit leave Sarah and enter my mother's body.

As families we fight, we harm each other; we blame each other, but we do not kill.

Sarah's pov

Running over to cables, I cradle him in my arms, tears dripping.

"I'm so sorry I got you involved. I love you."

Hearing coughing, I looked down.

"What was that? You love me" he chuckled.

"Git"

I punched him. "I thought you were dead."

With that, I kissed him, a lot. Once he was on his feet, I chucked his clothes from a nearby stone.

"Come on, let's get to Gloria."

Chapter 24

Gloria's pov

Sniffing the warmth of the air I climbed in a 4x4 Jeep Cherokee, and we headed north to where it was more barren. Taking as many weapons as we could, we told the other five vehicles to follow us. Driving along the road had me worried, it was too damn quiet. We all kept in radio contact, which Sarah had rigged up at an earlier date. When we heard gunshots, everyone stopped their vehicles to see where the shots were coming from. Then we noticed a small group of mutants running towards the forest, taking a closer look we saw four soldiers chasing then "fuck! I thought".

We could have just carried on, but I knew I couldn't just sit idly by. Telling the others we would meet them, we left. Getting Val to pull over. I went to the boot and gathered my two favorite swords and a machine gun for luck. Strapping them to my back, I smiled at Val.

"What, a girl needs her toys?"

Heading towards the forestry, it wasn't that hard to pick up the scent of mutants. They gave off a mixture of chemicals mixed up with whatever creature. Hearing a scream, Val was gone. Within seconds, he returned with a young man. Sniffing around him, I smiled.

"Another of the dog clan I'd say" I sniffed again "wolf I'd say."

The boy looked at Val, scared shitless to be fair.

"Don't worry, we won't hurt you. We're here to help."

That was that, the boy wouldn't shut the fuck up. He raved on about being taken from his family and how they had mixed his blood with that of a wolf.

"Shit, he's a werewolf."

I said out loud

"Really?" Gloria.

Val looked at me, shaking his head. I had read about them but never actually seen them around here.

"How many mutants escaped?"

"A few, but the soldiers killed them."

Walking back to the Jeep, I had an idea. I know how to get into the facility, and both I and Val smiled as we drove on.

The facility was huge, twice the size of the last place and twice as deep.

"How are we ever going to get through the large metal doors?" I said, "Let alone blow the whole place up?"

"There is a way the boy said nervously, but I'm not going back in. I'll draw you a map if that's okay." Val passed him a piece of paper and the boy drew the direction.

"Yuck," I said, "it's the garbage shoot."

"Yep, it's the only way in it's how we got out of the facility."

Pulling over, we left the boy in the Jeep, letting the others know what was happening. They kitted up for the time of their lives.

"Fuck that" I have a better way we'll just all mist in. There's always a small gap under the shutter doors, I'm not going down a garbage shoot." Val giggled.

Walking toward the facility I found myself worrying about what we would find there. Turning my head I saw a couple of people getting closer I was about to rip them apart until I realized it was Sarah and Cables.

Running up to Gloria, I wrapped my arms around her, I couldn't wait to tell her what had taken place. Watching his and Val's faces change to anger was not what I had expected.

"What they needed to talk about as a family."

"Fuck, what if they join forces? We will never have a chance," replied Gloria.

"Then we find a way to kill them all," replied Val with a serious look.

"What do you think the witches are talking about?" I said.

"I don't know, Sarah, but we have a plan and whatever happens; we have to take this facility," said Gloria.

"Everyone, if we can't blow the whole building we take it over" Gloria yelled.

Looking at Cables, I smiled

"In it till the end baby"

Taking the facility was a better idea. We could build our own safe house. It would be better for everyone, I thought. Holding on to Gloria, we misted and went under the shutter doors.

Anna's pov

As we traveled to the school, I looked up at the roof with the immense hole. "I will fix it," said Lucifer. Sitting down on a chair near the fire, I watched closely as Lucifer and the rest of my family talked. I watched as Lucifer spoke.

"Look, I'm sorry for everything I ever did to you and your sister. I had no right to hurt you," leaning over, he stroked my mother's face with his icy hand.

"So, how do we fix this mess? He said.

"We start again. We put things right, and that means changing what is happening in this city. Lucifer, we need to repair the damage you and I have done, and it starts with Dracula and his small team of extraordinary individuals. I mean, have you seen that wife of his? She is something special." replied Gabriel.

"I should think so." A woman's voice said.

They turned around to see Mercy standing there.

"I have something to say," We looked at her

"Gloria Val Dracula is my daughter. I brought her up as a child. If anyone touches her or Val, I will not be accountable for my actions and you, Lucifer, threaten me again. I will tell everyone who you are."

"Okay, I'm sorry, damn sis, I wouldn't off hurt her but you kept her a secret all these years."

"What? You didn't eat her like you did my boy from the village," replied Gabriel in a sarcastic tone.

Sit down please, Mercy Look, we're family and so are Gloria and Val to a point that, means we stand by them," replied Madelyn.

"Fuck, I never saw it that way," replied Lucifer.

"Okay, let's get this in order so we can at least start again as a family," I watched as everyone agreed.

"Anna, are you with us? We will help Gloria and Val and we then start again."

Standing, I ran over to them all with a cheesy grin on my face.

Margo's Pov

Listening, I realized something, I wanted to go home. This wasn't my fight anymore. I wanted to feel the wind on the peaks of the Scottish mountains. I wanted to be with my mother, picking herbs and not having to worry constantly.

"Madelyn"

"Yes sis, what wrong?"

"I want to go home back to Lochness."

I could feel her welling up.

"That means I'll never see you again."

"Not physically, but you will have me in your heart and my magic will be yours. I'm going to live again, go back, and start again. Look," she showed me a flashback of the Scottish mountains and our mother sitting on a rock, "always remember Madelyn, I love you."

Madelyn's pov

Feeling her spirit leave me was the worse pain I could face. Staring into space, I saw an image of my sister approaching our mother. Both were smiling as I watched my mother hug my sister, and a tear slid down my eye.

As my sister left, so did a part of my heart, but she left me with something quite remarkable, all of her powers.

Chapter 25

Gloria's Pov

Misting under the shutter doors, I knew we were facing an enormous challenge and it could cost us our lives. Dragging my swords as I walked made me feel alive with energy as the adrenaline pumped through my bloodstream.

Sometimes you have to dance with the devil to find the light.

Running in like lunatics at speed, we came to a massive experimental room. There were huge containers with what looked like human bodies growing in a mass of water. Looking at one of them closely made me jump as its eyes opened up.

"There must be a million pods here," I said.

Each had a specimen growing.

"Kill them all. No more fucking clones in our city."

Ripping their pipes, I watched as the machines started to shut down and the bodies twitch then I heard his Cables' father:

"If you destroy my life's work, I'll kill her."

Turning, I noticed Sarah was gone. Cables were lying knocked out on the floor.

"For fuck's sake," I said.

Sometimes your temper gets the best of you and we know where that leads.

Transforming, we took flight and set fire to the fucking lot. In the meantime, Cables had woken up.

Cables' pov

"Father, let her go. I don't want to do this."

"Son, you made your choice. Look around boy, this was the future, and now it's in flames.

"Where the heck do you think I got the money from to buy you all those cars and damn boy I could have let them kill you ages ago when you had turned into a half-breed mutt?"

Watching as he broke my girl's neck made me fall to the ground with despair, but soon anger took its place. Letting the monster out, I ran at him, knocking him flying.

Val's pov

Whilst Gloria went on her rampage I landed, changing back I knelt and lifted Sarah. "Cables she is yours, there's only one thing I can do, do you wish for it?" I could feel his pain, the sorrow in his heart. "Do it!" I screamed. Changing Sarah would take a little longer as she was already dead so I bit myself on the wrist and let my blood trickle into her mouth.

Cables' father's pov

Standing up, I brushed myself down. I watched as the bitch Gloria set my clones alight. Feeling my temper boil, I felt the change begin.

Cables pov

Watching my father change made me feel sick. "What was he becoming?" I yelled to Gloria before running over to Sarah. "Don't let him kill her and use the necklace, Val."

Gloria's pov

Transforming back I watched as a Cables' asshole father changed, what the fuck was that? It was a humongous scorpion and he was angry. Picking up my swords I stared at him before jumping in mid-air and landing on the creature, using its tail it flipped me, and I landed on my back.

"I'm coming!"

I heard Val shout, but it was too late, my head had gone I ran at the monster and skidded on the floor using my sword to cut its guts out, as it screamed in pain he used his tail and stabbed me in the shoulder pinning me up against a wall. Letting out a scream I watched Val jump on the monster, he was punching it multiple times but the monster flipped him with his other arm he sent Val flying, hitting a container. What the fuck? I thought we were going to die then it happened, Sarah was back and boy was she mean. She pounced on the creature's back whilst she grinned at me. She gripped the monster by the head and twisted it till we heard a snap. Letting go it fell to the ground, letting go of me as well. Sarah ran over to me, saying:

"That was fucking awesome. Did you see me ripping its head off just like that" looking at her, I stood up and wrapped my arms around her before I passed out.

Waking up, I lay down with my head on Val. Sarah and Cables were playing fighting. Looking at my shoulder, Val explained how I had been poisoned and how it had taken 16 hours for me to wake up.

"There you are", he said, "for a moment I thought I lost you."

Sitting up in the cartridge, I had a strange feeling it wasn't over.

Chapter 26

Gabriel's pov

So you think we should off intervene? Instead of watching? That Gloria needs an outlet, maybe we should have her and Val work for us.

"And the girl Sarah," Replied Lucifer.

"Well, considering what she has just done, she would make a great asset."

"And Cables."

"Hum, I don't know. I guess we could hire him as a bodyguard brother."

"When do we make a move?"

"Soon my brother."

Mercy's pov

I could off argued with my brothers when they told me their plans, but considering that my daughter and her team had already cleaned up a lot of our mess in this city, we were grateful. Even if my dick of a brother caused all the trouble, at least this way my brothers couldn't kill them, and to be honest, I don't think they would want to deal with all the stress. My daughter had a very aggressive side. So I volunteered to be the messenger and wait for the outcome.

Val's pov

Watching Gloria's fever grow made me question myself. I am worried sick. Can I save her? She was burning up, and it looked like her skin had a black infection, as it had traveled up her skin like a snake in slow motion.

"May I Help?"

Turning to see Mercy standing there. Kneeling, she touched Gloria's forehead.

"Oh, my child, what a mess you are in! I'm going to need a few things, Val. She's very ill, my boy."

Passing me a list of things, I realized it was going to take me to the coldest parts of the earth to find a special snowdrop petal. Telling Cables to keep Sarah in blood, I left to find the cure. Traveling to the northeast corner of the world, I faced many elements from the icy wind to the lack of human food. Living with animals was not my desired food, but what's a vampire to do? As I ate a small rodent creature, I looked up at the highest peak of a snow-covered mountain. And they're right at the edge was a small tuff of purple and white flowers. Climbing to the top, I picked the petals and placed them in a small bag. Worried sick about my wife, I transformed into a mist and left.

Mercy's pov

Softly I sang an ancient cradle song; it originated from the Scottish highlands. I told no one that our mother was born there.

The year was 1,020 ac, it was the middle ages. Times were hard, from what I can remember. As I child, the memory will always haunt me. It was a late night and I and my mother had just returned from a dance in Newhaven. On that particular night; my mother was smitten with a fine gentleman named Courbet.

Little did she know he belonged to an ancient family called the Van Lase, a religious cult that hunted creatures of the night? As I danced on the grass in the park, I watched as he sat next to her, she seemed so in love. Till I saw what he had in his hand, I wanted to scream but I hid instead, watching him kill my mother with a silver stake, breaking me. I wanted to tear him apart, but I couldn't let him find me. Two nights after my brothers found me in a grave crying telling them what happened, we knew we had to keep on moving.

Present-day

As I wiped her head Cables and Sarah cuddled up by the fire, singing the song, I realized I wasn't alone. Madelyn and Anna had arrived, looking at Gloria. We sang together.

Val's pov

Returning, I ran into the train station's cartridge, giving Mercy the ingredients.

"Are we ready, ladies?" mercy said.

"Can I join in? I've read the incantation?" said Sarah.

"She's over the blood lust."

Cables replies

"Okay, join us."

I watched as the ladies worked, mixing and saying a spell. I and Cables watched as the spell unfolded. Mercy poured a green liquid down Gloria's throat as we waited "Stand back it's going to get messy" she said.

Gloria's Pov

Waking up on a soft bed, I stretched.

"Good morning, my love. How did you sleep?"

"Beautiful my darling" I leaned over, kissing Val. I couldn't quite understand what was happening, was it all a dream? Jumping up out of bed, I went to the dressing room mirror and opened my mouth. No fangs. I was human.

"What are you doing?"

Val looked at me inquisitively.

"Nothing loves."

I gripped the hairbrush and brushed my hair. Sitting down, I couldn't quite believe where I was. Hector came running in.

"Mother, you've been gone a long time. I've been waiting for you". Giving him love, I stood up and walked to the window, pulling the curtains open. I saw a man who looked like Cables playing piano and my mother was singing. I couldn't quite understand what was happening in this world, but I was happy.

Looking at my son laughing with his father, I looked in the mirror and noticed something terrible. He didn't have a reflection he simply wasn't there. Turning to face Hector, I watched as his face grew paler and his fangs came out.

"What's wrong mummy, don't you love me anymore? You said I would live forever mother, his words dragged on, and the room spun.

I went to scream, but nothing was coming out. It was like my horrors and my happy place were infolding on themselves.

"No", my head kept saying, not my son please he's just a boy.

Falling into a bottomless well, I felt my throat fill up with water. I was drowning, and then I heard:

"Hold her up, she's going to puke," I heard Val say.

"That's horrid."

Said Sarah as lots of black oozes came up out of my throat.

"Fuck shit, that was the worse dream ever."

Sitting up, I looked around.

"What, you have never seen someone puke before?" Sarah burst out laughing and so did everyone else. Val sat next to me and whispered, "I was so scared to lose you."

Sarah's pov

Whilst everyone sat around talking, I slipped out. There was a part of me that egged me on to face my real father and I needed to find out the reason he did what he did.

Chapter 27

Lucifer's pov

I couldn't believe all my plans had gone up in smoke; I really couldn't believe a newbie vampire could kill, like a professional assassin. Smirking to myself, I grabbed myself a glass of whisky

"Father"

I heard turning around to find Anna standing there.

"We need to talk."

"She took to a seat, and she looked at me in a serious tone."

"Why did you do it? I want to know why you hit her. She loved you and you hurt her>"

"It was a long time ago Anna. Do you want to know what happened?"

"Yes, I need to have a clear picture; my other father never told me what happened. I saw some of it in a vision."

"You have visions? You never told me that."

"I told no one."

"Okay, the year it happened, it was your 6th birthday. I loved you so much and the way your mother brushed your long brown hair in the moonlight, but we were concerned about your lust for human blood and how it controlled you. We would take you out nightly to feed on the wayward and strays of the city, but this one night, the local village held a dance. They were singing and dancing to the moon whilst a great fire burned. You had wanted so much to join in with the other children, but we couldn't allow it. Putting you to bed, I went out to hunt.

When you slipped out without your mother knowing, my temper got the best of me. I screamed at her, blaming her for everything, and stormed out. I looked everywhere traveling the cities, high and low, and when I went to tell my family what had happened, you had changed into an adult.

Gabriel said he had found you wondering about the village and had adopted you. So I left and turned to the taverns asking questions. I had stopped eating, and the lust took over me. I felt an intense rage inside of me. I was so depressed I blamed the one person I loved the most, your mother. I wish I never hit her. When I returned one night I found her gone, the place had been ransacked. Moving back in with my brother and sister was all I could do, but a part of me resented my brother so I became bitter and twisted and I loved it.

Anna's pov

"My father said he found me wandering around and that a witch had wiped my memory, yet when my Mother got in touch I remember it as a vision."

"I'm sorry, how did Gabriel teach you to control your temper?"

"He"

I didn't want to remember, but the visions showed me. "I was 18, and I was in a large training room. If I could complete the obstacles Gabriel had set for me, I would eat, but if I didn't, he would leave me to starve, so I learned to adapt and promised myself I would get out of there when I could."

"It makes sense."

I wanted to cry, but I was strong, so I put a barrier up to stop the memory. Walking out of the room, I said goodnight. I was still worried about Gloria and her friends and I still didn't trust Lucifer, my father. There was something about his story. He said he loved the evilness of his mood that was crazy in itself. Going over things in my mind I felt a sudden urge to explode, I was sick of keeping everything bottled up. Both my parents had abused me and I knew what I had to do and it was going to be nice. I was tired of being a vampire pleaser, I was a hybrid, and that alone made me different.

Walking into my room, I broke a wooden chair, picking up a leg. I sat down and used a pocketknife from out of my dressing table drawer and I sharpened the wood, all the time singing a song. Sometimes a girl's got to do what a girl's got to do, and I wanted my parents dead.

Killing Lucifer there and then would have been too easy; I wanted him to suffer for what he did. Putting some clothes and the stake in a rucksack, I decided there and then I was walking away. Jumping into one of the black 4x4 Jeeps, I looked around for the key. Flipping the sunshade down, I found the keys there. Driving away into the night, I knew I had to find a place to stay. Thinking of all the places, I realized something. I was alone in this world and no one would ever fuck with me again. Driving, I came past an old cinema house. It was boarded up with wood and covered in graffiti. This would have to do. It wasn't a bad place just needed a little clean-up here and there. Looking at the stage covered in dust and old furniture I took to cleaning and moving things about I thought about the others and I knew I would have to put a blocking spell up as I didn't want anyone to find me, especially Lucifer.

Lucifer's Pov

Feeling stressed after my and Anna's talk, I thought I would go check on her. I didn't want her to feel like I never loved her. Pushing her door open, I noticed she was gone and so were her belongings, shit I thought, I had to find her before her mother killed me. Leaving, I picked up the scent of petrol in the air. Running to the garage, I thought, fuck, she had only taken my best Jeep. Yes, I was a vampire, and I loved the thrill of the chase, but I was still a man and I loved my toys. Going back outside I turned into a mist and followed the tracks that the Jeep had left, but soon as I hit the open road I had to use my senses, and picking up Anna's scent was impossible. Why was that? Then I realized she had used a cloaking spell to stop me from finding her. As I traveled, I realized someone was with me.

"You lost her again?"

I thought I heard a woman say "Oh shit". Stopping dead I transformed back into my normal self.

"Okay, Madelyn, don't be angry. It wasn't my fault. She asked me for the entire story so I told her."

Madelyn stood there with her arms crossed.

"So, what's the plan I said?"

"You", she prodded me with her finger. "What did you do?"

"Nothing. I promise I never touched her. I wouldn't"

We sat down on a log to talk.

"Look Madelyn, I'm sorry I hurt you. I don't know why I couldn't control my anger. It was like I had a volcano inside me."

I went to speak again, but she punched me in the jaw with her fist. She was shaking like crazy. "Do you know the damage you caused? You took my love and turned it to hatred, yet as I stand here now fuming I want to fuck you."

Damn, she kissed me with tongue and all. Stopping, we stared at each other, and then we kissed again. Standing up, I gripped her and pushed her against a tree. The roughness of the tree made it more sensual. Lifting her blue dress, I felt her soft warm legs fuck I thought, I had missed this so much. It was then she demanded I fucked her there and then. Unzipping my trousers, she gripped my hard cock and kissed me as I inserted myself into her. Harder and harder, I pushed as she let out a moan of pleasure. The hitting of the tree only helped with the pleasure we were in. Hearing a cough come from behind, I pivoted my head.

"Brother, I see you and Madelyn have made up."

"You couldn't have waited, for 5 more minutes for me to finish?"

"Well, you know I love a little watch, my brother. Now for the reason, I'm here. Where is my daughter?"

After I and Madelyn had straightened ourselves out, I explained myself.

"So, you put your foot in it again."

"Yeah, sorry I have, but it wasn't planned, my brother."

I watched as my brother turned to Madelyn and smiled

"Hello my dear, shall we sort this mess out? I'll talk to my brother, and then I'll go home and grab a few things we may need."

Madelyn's pov

I wanted to walk away from him, but love never really leaves. Even if you say you hate them, you remember the good times you had with them. We did have a child, Anna, together. While I listened to Lucifer and Gabriel talk, I worried about Anna. Why did she go? What caused her to be so angry about leaving? I tried to connect to her, but she had blocked me.

"Stop, I have an idea. I need to do a spell but you both need to get out of the way from the blast it gives off."

Surely I could find her and connect. Kneeling, I listened to the ground and used its energy to send a massive force of electricity to unblock Anna's magic.

Watching Gabriel leave, I tried to connect with my daughter.

"Anna, please, it's me. We only want to talk."

Nothing, not even a whisper. It was then Gloria made contact.

"Madelyn, it's me, Gloria. I just wanted to say thank you."

I didn't expect to break down and cry like a baby, but I was worried sick, so I told Gloria everything.

Chapter 28

Gloria's pov

After listening to what Madelyn told me, I felt so sorry. I know it wasn't my business, but for the last few weeks, we had been involved in each other's business to the point I nearly died.

"Fuck it," I said, standing up and wobbling over to the fridge.

"Sit down; you're not ready to be running around." I heard Val say. Passing me a blood bag of A-Positive, I noticed Sarah was staring at me.

"What's wrong?"

"Will the blood lust ever go? It's not like I want to rip someone apart, but it's all I think about, the blood, I mean."

"It fades"

I said as I shared my blood bag with her. As I sat there, I told everyone what was happening with Anna and the amount of shit Lucifer had caused. But was I ready to fight again? Looking around the room, I noticed Cables seemed rather quiet. I already knew he was feeling low after losing his father, so I approached him.

"Cables, I'm sorry how things went down."

"Don't be. He was a wanker and a bully. Do we have time to listen to a story about my childhood?"

Why not? I thought. I wasn't feeling a hundred present anyway, so I sat back down and we all listened.

Cables' pov

I was ten years old when my father sent me to stay with my great-grandparents. It was winter, and the snow had fallen deeper than I have ever seen. Waking up to see another boy in my room took me by surprise. He told me his name was Timothy, and he was the son of a famous singer and he was there to learn how to be a gentleman. We became friends but there was something not right about him, he always loved to talk about death and the art of the dark occults. One morning I awoke to find something unusual, my maid Clara was dead, suspended in mid-air with blood dripping from her neck. Running to my grandfather to cry I was pushed and told to grow up and face death like a man. That night, I heard Timothy talking to someone. As I lay there in the dark, I knew he was not normal.

"Wake up," I felt timothy pushing me.

Look, I have to tell you you're not safe here. There's only so much I can do. I've been trying to use the white magic to protect us, but he comes at night whilst we sleep.

"Who comes?" I said, pretending that I didn't know.

"Do I have to spell it out? He's names Lucifer. He a bloody vampire."

"A vampire" I repeated.

"I thought they weren't real, well how the heck did the maid hang like that?"

"What we saw was a mirror reflection and you know vampires don't have any reflection at all."

Sitting up in bed, I asked him straight,

"Look, I saw you talking to someone."

"Yes, my book. Her name's Madelyn. She was telling me how to protect ourselves here take this."

He passed me a couple of stakes and a hammer.

"Look, we have to go to the graveyard. We have to kill her before she rises."

"Who," I said stupidly.

"The maid's a creature of the night now, get dressed."

"What about Lucifer?"

He can't touch us. Madelyn says she knows him and he won't hurt children."

"How does she know that?"

"I'm not supposed to say, but she was once married to him a long time ago. Now come on."

Getting dressed, we sneaked downstairs past my grandfather, who was asleep in his armchair. He was ancient-fashioned in his ways, but I knew he cared about me to a degree. I heard him telling my father how beating me would never make me a man and that I needed care and affection. That's how I ended up here; my father was a brute of a man. Opening the door, we tiptoed out. The night was bitter, and the snow was still falling, living near a graveyard had always scared me.

"This way," Timothy said.

Feeling scared out of my wits, we entered the church where her coffin lay. The church itself was old, with its painted glass windows and the vines that grew up on the sides of the old brickwork. Moving closer, I gripped hold of a stake and hammer and my heart was pounding fast. "Are you ready? When I say stab her"

"Why cart you do it?" I said.

"Because you're bigger than me," Timothy replied.

Lifting the coffin was nerve-racking, but to our disappointment, the coffin was empty. For a split second, we froze, looking at each other in shock. Where was she? Turning to walk out, she came from behind the holder. Eyes red as hell and sharp, pointy teeth. We tried to run, but she was fast. Screaming, I hid, but she found me and lifted me into the air. To my amazement, I saw a stake go straight through her heart and she dropped to the ground.

"Now stay dead, fucking vampires" looking at my Grandfather I couldn't help but smile. He was a fucking god damn vampire hunter. Going back to the house, he told us to stay in our room. That same night, we sneaked downstairs, overhearing my grandfather and another gentleman talking. They were talking about setting traps and making the grounds safe. With that, I guessed they meant holy water and garlic.

"Fuck shit Cables, that's some serious stuff to go through. What happened to the boy?" Gloria replied.

"He left the following morning. I was told his parents transferred him to a new school. Some monks collected him; they called themselves the brotherhood of something. What about your grandfather?"

"He passed away on my 12th birthday. They said he had a heart attack, but I have my suspicions."

"I'm guessing it was Lucifer," said Val.

"What a bitch said, Sarah. We all stared at her, and she was eating a piece of raw steak.

Sarah's pov

Sitting there listening to Cables made me realize something, I'm going to live forever unless some old sod comes along and stakes me, then that would be a total bummer. Looking at Cables got me thinking about my childhood, if blabbing was a thing I would be top of my class.

"My mother was an alcoholic and my dad; well left us when I was small. We lived in an old trailer park, I told no one. I ran away from home and was found by a nun her name was Celia she took me in but I was unruly and kept running away. I was then introduced to the Brotherhood. They taught me how to fight and when I finally was introduced to a famous brother of the truth, he just happened to be my father. Bursting out crying, I sank into the sofa, Cables sat next to me and wrapped his arms around me.

"Gloria, I think we should go find Anna. It would take Cables and Sarah's minds off things," said Val.

Leaving to hunt for Anna was our best choice; everyone had gone through so much shit we needed it all to end. Sniffing the air, I smelt nothing but leftover vamp meat.

"Thank you, Sarah, for eating that steak."

"Oh, I heard that, Sorry Sarah," I said giggling, as I got in the car with Val.

"Val, you think we were doing the right thing? Maybe Anna doesn't want to be found?"

"Well, in that case, maybe we should just find a way to make her come home."

Driving away, I gripped Val's hand.

"Are you crying?" he said.

"No babes, it's just I'm worrying a bit."

"Why? I'm sure she was safe."

"I haven't heard from my mother and I've only just found her."

He gripped my hand tighter

"Don't worry, she will be in contact."

Mercy's pov

I know I told my brother Lucifer about Gloria, but I had a feeling he would not let it die. He had a way of poking at a dead horse over and over. I was worried sick, but what could I do?

Going to check on my brother's coffins, I noticed they weren't in, so to speak I noticed one thing though; Lucifer had only forgotten his ring. Slipping in on my finger, I smiled to myself. How was that, gave mine away just to find another? I always wanted to go to the beach. It had been years since I paddled in the cold seawater. Waiting for the morning sunlight, I had a strange feeling Gloria was in trouble. Shit. I knew then I had to leave.

"Gloria, are you okay?"

"I am now," she replied.

I was worried sick. "I'm sorry, my darling, I had to do something."

"What!" she said. Well, okay, I'm paddling in the ocean telling my daughter about their ring"

She giggled.

"Now tell me what's going on."

Listening to what had happened, I felt shocked to find out that my daughter nearly died and on top of that, Anna had taken off. Poor Anna, I thought, where was she? I knew I could help her if I only knew where to look.

Anna's pov

As I cleaned the old cinema seats, I couldn't help but feel a presence watching me. Turning I saw Gabriel standing there, was' an unusual sight. My father had a way of creeping up on me.

"Father, I need space."

"I know my daughter; I'm not completely without emotions. I can read your emotions

"Sit down, Anna; we need to have a chat. Look, if you going to take my brother on, you will need help, or eventually, he will kill you, whether you are his daughter or not."

Looking at him, I had to play to his words, as I wasn't prepared to kill him just yet. Wrapping my arms around, him I sobbed.

"I can't go back, I won't."

"I know, so I'm going to help you. Revenge my daughter is best served cold. Especially where my brother is concerned."

Lucifer's Pov

Watching my brother leave, I sat next to Madelyn for once. I felt needed and loved. Could I control the beast inside of me? Sitting there, we both agreed to get our family back was a priority, but first, we had to find our daughter.

Anna's pov

Making a deal with my father was not the first option. I blamed him as well for his part in my upbringing. Watching Gabriel leave I knew I was going to have to bring out the real me I was sick of pretending I was a full vampire when infect I was half-witch. That gave me an idea; I wanted to see where everyone was so I pulled out an old map and an old chain with a clear diamond on the end which I had kept in my rucksack. Saying a few words, I asked it to show me where Lucifer was. The stone had its way of giving me images like picture slides from times past. Watching Lucifer sit next to my mother kissing her made my blood boil. How could she forgive him?

"Mother!"

I screamed, feeling an urge to want to rip things apart I started to throw chairs and tables across the room.

Sitting down on the dirty floor I cried, what was I doing, where was my life heading? Everyone has a story but I was lonely I was brought up in an abandoned school and never allowed to make friends with anyone. As I wiped my tears, I thought I heard rustling coming from behind a chair. Walking over, I came across someone, a small boy with mousy brown hair. He must have been about 11.

"Hello, who are you?" The boy looked scared, but the way he was dressed was from times gone by and I mean 200 years ago!

"My name is Hector. I don't know where I am. One minute I was with my mammy and daddy and then it was dark"

"So how did you get here?" "I don't know"

He put his head down. Wrapping my arms around him, I spoke softly:

"Don't worry; I'll be your family".

The boy smiled.

"Will you find my daddy and mummy?"

"What are their names?"

"My daddy's name is Val and my mother is Gloria. Have you seen them?" he burst out crying.

Shit, all I could think about was my friends and were they his parents. How though? Their son had died years ago? Magic, I guessed in the end or some alien had opened up another dimension and he just happened to walk in. Either way, I had to get in touch with Gloria and Val.

Gloria's pov

As we drove on singing away to the classic rock cd, I had a feeling Anna was nearby.

"Stop the car Val, I can hear her."

"Strangely enough, I was just about to say the same."

Jumping out of the car, we came to an ancient cinema and opened the door we looked in, "Anna, you in here" I said.

Anna walked out from behind a long red curtain, but she wasn't alone. She had a small boy. He looked up at me and ran.

"Mummy, Daddy"

"Val is that hector? But how?"

Finding myself crying, I sniffed at the boy. He smelt like our boy; he felt like our boy.

"He's real, but he displaced in time," Val said as I hugged Hector

"Father"

He said as Val took him from me and cuddled him in his arms.

"I missed you both so much. School is so hard, Father."

Sitting down at the table, Hector went to talk to Anna.

Someone has opened a space-time portal, Gloria. There's only one person who can do that, and that's Margo. Whilst hector played hide and seek, I noticed a little paper on the floor. Kneeling, I picked it up and read it.

Gloria and Val, I wanted to give you something back for being my friend so I thought I   would return what you had lost love you both happy families, your Margo.

Crying, I fell to the floor. So good things do happen.

"Anna, thank you."

Anna looked at me and I knew she wanted to talk with me alone.

"Val, look after Hector." Kissing him, I walked off with Anna.

"What going on Anna?"

Anna looked like she had been sobbing.

"I thought running away would make it easier. I'm so sick of being in the course of all this trouble. Look at them. I have a monster for a father and a mother who's scared of her own shadow, and I want it to stop. I want my mother to see the real Lucifer for what he is. I'm going to make him pay for all the shit he's caused us, and I know he loved causing it all. As he told me in his own words, so I've decided I'm going to kill him, and then I and my mother can be free."

I didn't know what to say, so leaning in; I wrapped my arms around her and whispered we are with you on this. Lucifer will pay, just like Cables' Father did my girl.

Cables' pov

I couldn't quite believe what had taken place. Driving along a dark narrow road in search of Anna, I noticed a Jeep following us.

"Strap in Sarah," I said.

"We're being followed and I don't think it's something good" driving faster I watched as the vehicle disappeared. I think we were safe now and then it happened, the black Jeep smashed into us, and it was like slow motion watching ourselves repeatedly roll over in the mud. Landing upside down, I turned to Sarah, but she was knocked out cold from the impact of the blunt force. Dragging myself out of the window, I noticed my right leg had a pipe going straight through it. I pulled it out, letting out a scream. Sarah, I spoke as I coughed up blood. She had started to stir.

"What going on? Who hit us?" Sarah replied.

"I don't know but there's a few of them. Come on let's get out of here."

"I can't, I'm trapped."

"Well, use your fucking vampire strength and climb the fuck out of there."

Sarah looked at me as if she was going to rip me apart. Watching her eyes change to a more darkened red, I saw the change taking place. Her temper was wild, tearing the seats apart she clambered out of the car and stared at me with daggers, I thought she was going to kill me but she jumped out and ran towards the other vehicle like a rampaging lunatic and fuck was she sexy. Watching my girl drag the driver out of the Jeep, she let out a high-pitched scream of pure sexual anger. While she ripped and ate, I grabbed the other person. He was trying to run off, but I caught him. "Who sent you? Why did you hit us off the road?" It grinned and spat blood. "Tell me now" I yelled. Coughing up blood, his final words were:

"Your father sent us."

"But he's dead."

The guy giggled.

"You really think he didn't have another backup of himself? He's one step in front of you" he let out a spur of blood and died there in my hands. Dropping him, I sank to the floor. Well, fuck me, it was only the beginning. Sarah came over wiping her mouth "

"So we go on a mission but this time we come well prepared" She smiled at me and we walked.

"Gather you're not hungry then," I said. She giggled and gave me a nudge.

"So who's telling Val?"

We both stared at each other and it was one of those moments where you point at each other and say I'm not doing it, you can.

Val's pov

Having our son back meant we could be a family again. Gloria seemed so happy, as I watched her playing with Hector and Anna Who knew where she was heading. Listening to Anna and my wife chat. I knew Anna would never be totally happy with all that had happened. Would she be able to catch him?

For a start, he was stronger than her and faster and he was older but she had magic that gave me an idea. What if we trapped him? We could chain him up and drop him at the bottom of the sea? All the time, he would live in his memory. He would never realize what was happening, but how was I to do this?

"I can do that."

Heard Anna behind me.

"I know of a spell we can use. If we can't kill him, surely we can make him suffer for hundreds of years."

"Anna, do you know what this would mean?"

"Yes, letting my guard down, pretending to be his daughter, at least until we have him, and telling Gloria what was going to happen. I made sure she took Hector to the Brotherhood and told them to keep both our boys safe.

Anna's pov

Dropping the spell from my doors, I sat and waited for my so-called family to find me. Seeing them walk through the doors, I put on the waterworks.

"Mother, I'm sorry, I felt so lost, I thought I needed space to understand, now I see." We talked for hours, Lucifer, my mother, and I. Watching my mother go to fetch blood for my father, I spoke in a soft neutral manner, "father I'm sorry you lost me. I didn't know I was a course so much pain."

Cuddling him, I whisper a dark spell that had him trapped in a moment in time, watching him sit there and stare. My mother came back with the blood.

"What have you done?"

"Mother, he lied to you. He told me he enjoyed hurting you. I replayed the conversation to her so she could watch everything. Watching her face grow angrier, she looked at him and said:

"Quick, we need to be quick, we need to run."

"No, mother, we have to finish this."

Yelling to Val to bring out the chains, I watched my mother perform a binding spell on it. It was so strong it would take a thousand elephants to break the spell. Wrapping the chains around Lucifer, I watched as Val went to mist.

"Wait, I'm coming" as we demised by the ocean, I whispered into my father's ear:

"It's for your safety."

His eyes flickered but he couldn't move because of the memory he was living. Using a boat we headed out to sea. Dropping his body into the sea, we watched it sink as the deep waters took him. So did my hatred leave with him?

"Val, I want to go someplace where nobody knows me, I want me and my mother to be happy."

Val looked at me. By the time we got back to the harbor, Gabriel was standing there with Gloria and my mother. He smiled.

Val's Pov,

I knew what I had to do. Holding on to the bracelet with Gloria nodding I gave it to Gabriel and let them go home. Gabriel, it's our world not there's. Watching Gabriel tell Anna and her mother made me smile. As they pressed the bracelets stone, I watched as they went through the portal.

"Go Gabriel, she's your daughter as well. See you in a few hundred years," he turned and grinned, for once he seemed happy.

Walking away for a moment, we were happy until Cables, and Sarah ran up to us. "He's fucking still alive!"

"Who?" I said.

"Cables' father."

Gloria pov

"Well, you know what that means. It's time to get the enormous swords out." We walked away as if it was just another fucking night.

Printed in Great Britain
by Amazon

84198682R00129